SOUTHGATE VETERANS
MEMORIAL LIBRARY
14680 DIX-TOLEDO ROAD
SOUTHGATE, MI 48195

P9-DNB-157

Something to Sing About

DATE DUE		
JAN 2 6 2009	NOV 0 9 2016	
FEB 2 3 2009		
MAR 1 4 2009		
JUN 3 0 2009		
JUL 2 2 2009		
AUG 1 2 2009		
AUG 2 9 2011		

SOUTHGATE VETERANS
MEMORIAL LIBRARY
14680 DIX-TOLEDO ROAD
SOUTHGATE, MI 48195

Something to Sing About

Written by

C. C. Payne

Eerdmans Books for Young Readers
Grand Rapids, Michigan / Cambridge, U.K.

SOUTHGATE VETERANS
MEMORIAL LIBRARY
14680 DIX-TOLEDO ROAD
SOUTHGATE, MI 48195

Copyright © 2008 Eerdmans Books for Young Readers,
an imprint of Wm. B. Eerdmans Publishing Co.
All rights reserved

Wm. B. Eerdmans Publishing Co.
2140 Oak Industrial Dr. N.E., Grand Rapids, Michigan 49505
P.O. Box 163, Cambridge CB3 9PU U.K.
www.eerdmans.com/youngreaders

Printed in the United States of America

08 09 10 11 12 13 14   7 6 5 4 3 2 1

Library of Congress Cataloging-in-Publication Data

Payne, Catherine Clark.
Something to sing about / by Catherine Clark Payne.
p.   cm.
Summary: Ten-year-old Jamie Jo's fear of bees keeps her inside
most of the time, but a series of events that begins when her mother
is excluded from the church choir brings about many changes,
including new friendships and greater trust in God.

ISBN 978-0-8028-5344-8 (alk. paper)

[1. Phobias — Fiction. 2. Bees — Fiction. 3. Family life —
Kentucky — Fiction. 4. Neighbors — Fiction. 5. Christian life —
Fiction. 6. Choirs (Music) — Fiction. 7. Singing — Fiction.
8. Kentucky — Fiction.] I. Title.
PZ7.P2942Som   2008
[Fic] — dc22
2008006100

3 9082 10820 1727

In loving memories of

Roy & Ruth Lanphear
Harold Dean Payne
Kenneth Fife Payne
Timothy Dean Payne
& Joseph E. Stopher

Though they've soared beyond our reach,
they've left us with plenty to sing about.

Contents

Chapter One

"Jamie Jo Morgan, you have to the count of ten to get down here, or I'm leaving without you!" Mama hollered from the front porch.

It was 6:03 on Wednesday evening, May 29th. I always know precisely what day and time it is, because my older brother, Pate, gave me a wristwatch from the Dollar General store that tells me so.

"One!"

Anyway, 6:03, that's precisely when I began to panic. I panicked because I *am* Jamie Jo Morgan, and I didn't want to be left at home. But I couldn't find my other sandal!

"Two!"

Now I know lots of parents who count like this,

but would never actually leave their children behind. Mama isn't one of those pretend-counters. She really will leave the house without me, especially if she's on her way to church — which she was.

"Three!"

I ran through the house with one sandal on, bending and spinning, pulling back drapes and looking under furniture. My footsteps *click-slap click-slapped* against the old wooden plank floors.

"Four!"

Mama never missed church and she was never late, no matter what. Never. In her mind, she once told me, it was like she had an appointment with The Lord. Now don't get me wrong: If I had an appointment with The Lord, I'd be on time for it, too. I have a lot of questions for him.

"Five!"

But I'd been going to church my whole life, and I'd never once bumped into The Lord there. (Mama said that's because I wasn't looking, but I was, I tell you!) So, my reasons for wanting to go to church were different from Mama's. Churchin' is pretty much the one and only regular social activity around here. Of course, they don't use the word "social"; they say "fellowship," which means the same thing but is more churchy.

"Six!"

I live in Franklin, Kentucky, population: 8,079. Eight thousand sounds like a lot of people, doesn't it? It isn't, not compared to other cities. New York City, for example, has a population of eight *million.* See what I mean?

"Seven!"

Anyway, of the eight thousand or so people who live here, I'd guess that at least half of them are farmers. If you ask me, farmers are the hardest-working people on the planet. Farmers work and work and work, and then they work some more. They have the whole world to feed, after all. There are only two things I know of that bring farmers in from the fields: rain and church. So, church is big around here.

"Eight!"

Found it! I yanked my sandal out from under the dog bed. I don't have a dog, just a dog bed . . . and a dog collar, a leash, some dog dishes, a dog-training book.

"Nine!"

I slipped the sandal on, ran down the stairs, and burst out onto the front porch. The screen door screeched and slapped shut behind me.

Mama smiled. "I almost left without you."

"I know."

If Mama had left without me, then I might've had to wait three whole days for another chance to get out of the house. I wouldn't get out 'til church on Sunday morning.

Mostly, I considered this Daddy's fault. We only had one truck, and Daddy drove it to work in Bowling Green, the next town over. Daddy is a prosecuting attorney, which means that he helps to put people who have committed crimes in jail.

Mama stays home, and insists that she doesn't need or want a car of her own. "Isn't that one of the benefits of living downtown?" she always says. "Everything I need is right here, within walking distance: clothing stores, the beauty shop, the drugstore, the coffee shop, the bakery, church . . ."

It's true, but walking isn't always convenient,

especially when you take into account the changing seasons and weather.

But we walked anyway. We walked even on the weekends, because of Daddy's rule: once the truck was parked in the driveway at 5:30 on Friday, it wasn't supposed to move again until Monday morning at 7:30.

Last week the sky had poured rain for four days straight, so Mama and I had stayed in the house for four days straight. By Friday afternoon, we were going crazy. We watched for Daddy's truck through the front window and rushed outside as soon as we saw it.

We caught Daddy in the driveway at 4:27, before he'd even turned the engine off. "Please, Daddy," I begged, "Can we go — "

But he was already shaking his head. "The truck's already parked," he said. Then he pointed to the P on the dashboard with a little orange circle around it. "P stands for Park."

Now, does that sound like any kind of a reason to you? It doesn't to me, either. At that moment, I understood what Mama meant when she said that Daddy was as stubborn as a mule. He was stubborn about his clothes, his truck, his food — he won't even *taste* anything with nuts in it! Yup, my daddy is just plain stubborn about *everything*.

But to be fair, I have my own rule: I never go outside without Mama. I could if I wanted to — I am ten years old, after all! I just don't want to, because I'm a teensy, weensy, little bitty bit, afraid of bees. Okay, okay, the truth is that I am *deathly* afraid of bees.

That's why Mama carries a lime-green flyswatter everywhere we go (by now, that thing is like a natural part of her hand) and that's how she became The Bee Slayer. Whenever bees come near me, Mama swats them away, almost always *before* I start screaming.

I've never been attacked by a whole hive of bees or anything awful like that. In fact, I've never even been stung, not once! I just want to keep it that way is all. Granted, I don't know *exactly* what would happen if a bee stung me, what it would look like and feel like and be like. But I do know that I would eventually die from the bee sting. And I don't mean die in a dramatic *Oh-I-would-just-die-if-that-ever-happened-to-me* way. I mean *die,* as in *death.* I am a highly sensitive person!

Just about everything gives me a rash. I have to use special soaps and lotions made for highly sensitive people like me. I have to cover the little silver snap on the insides of my jeans with a Band-Aid — or it gives me a rash. And the problems I have with toilet paper. If I use any kind of colored or perfumed toilet paper, I have fire-pee! (This is when your urine feels like fire shooting out of your body.)

Even the sun bothers me. It doesn't exactly give me a rash, but it doesn't exactly give me a tan either. Mama says I have a sunning process: freckle, burn, peel.

Anyhow, the sun didn't look like it would bother me tonight. It was hiding somewhere behind the clouds — but it was still hot! And so far I didn't see any bees. If one came along on the way to church, Mama would be there with her flyswatter.

I was already sticky and sweaty when we started down the steps toward the sidewalk. I smoothed my purple sundress with my hands, and wondered if my hair was completely wrecked. I hadn't had time to look in the mirror.

As if reading my mind, Mama said, "Your hair looks perfectly beautiful, Jamie Jo."

My stomach did a flip. I hadn't been going for "beautiful." Beautiful stands out. I know, because my mother is beautiful, and people stare at her wherever we go. (Mama doesn't seem to notice.)

But *I* notice, and I don't like people staring at me. I don't want to stand out in any way, bad *or* good.

I thought about this while Mama pointed at flowers with her flyswatter: "Look at those climbing roses, Jamie Jo. And those lilies . . ."

"Uh-huh," I said, when it seemed like Mama was waiting for me to say something.

It was the flower, I knew, that had put my hair over the top into the "beautiful" category. I'd tried to talk Mama out of putting the flower in my hair (bees like flowers!) but she'd been determined. Mama was as proud of the long, blond ponytail she'd made on one side of my head as she was of the soft-white peony she'd grown on the side of our house.

8

I decided to ditch the flower as soon as we got to church, before anybody saw me. If Mama asked me about it later, I'd pretend I didn't know that it had fallen out.

"Can we stop by the drugstore on the way?" I asked. I was really hot and getting thirsty. The drug-store had both air-conditioning and a soda fountain.

"We can't *now*. You took too long getting ready, Jamie Jo. Now we're late," Mama said matter-of-factly, and then, "Ooooh! Look at that hydrangea."

"Uh-huh."

We weren't late. In fact, I was pretty sure that we were still *early*. Mama is always early for choir prac-tice. In fact, she's always the first person to arrive. She even gets there before the choir director, Mrs. Snopes. The only explanation I have is this: my mama *loves* to sing and it doesn't bother her one bit that she isn't very good at it.

Once, several years ago, Pate and I had decided to tell Mama that she was a bad singer. It was Pate's idea, and he acted like he was really doing Mama (and everybody else) a big favor. I thought it would be nice to do Mama a favor, too.

So, we cornered her in the kitchen one Sunday afternoon after a particularly loud, particularly *bad* performance at church.

Pate did the talking. At first he hemmed and hawed, but finally he stammered, "Uh, Mama, you're not exactly the best singer in the choir, not *exactly,* you know?"

Mama laughed. "Yes, I know, Pate," she said. "I'm definitely the worst."

Pate and I just blinked at each other, surprised and confused.

Then Mama turned from the sink to look at the both of us. "For me, the joy of singing is in the doing, not in the results."

We still didn't understand.

"Pate, were you good at the guitar the first time you picked it up?" Mama asked.

"No, ma'am," Pate said honestly.

"But the joy was in the doing, so you kept on doing, and you got better, right?" Mama said.

Very slowly, Pate said, "Riiiiiight."

I knew what he was thinking. Mama wasn't getting any better at singing, and she'd been doing it for a very long time.

"What about you, Jamie Jo?" Mama said. "You'd still love math even if you weren't great at it, right?"

"No," I said. "I'd hate it. I like it *because* I'm good at it."

Mama had just laughed and thrown her hands up in the air.

Now she was talking about flowers again. "And those daisies . . ."

"Uh-huh," I said, wiping sweat off my forehead with the back of my hand. "Did you even ask Daddy if we could take the truck to church?"

"Walking is good for us, Jamie Jo. It gives us time to drink in the beauty all around us. You can't do that when you're zooming past everything in a car."

I took that as a *no.* I had a sneaking suspicion that Mama really liked to walk. I didn't.

When we arrived at church, I left Mama at the door to the choir room, which was still dark and empty, and headed for the nearest bathroom to ditch the flower.

I hadn't thought that there might be other girls in the bathroom. I also hadn't thought that they hated me. In fact, I hadn't thought that these particular girls even knew I existed, much less knew me well enough to hate me. But it turned out that I was wrong about a lot of things.

As soon as I walked into the ladies room, Michelle Snopes and Katie Lynn Howard rolled their eyes and smirked at each other in the mirror.

"Nice flower," Katie Lynn said, giggling.

Michelle seemed to consider me in the mirror as she rubbed her glossy lips together. Then she turned her back on the mirror to face me. "Actually, I don't like it," she said. She took a step toward me and looked me up and down. She took her time inspecting the flower, my hair, my dress, and my shoes.

I was too shocked to move or speak, so I just stood there, trying to understand what was happening.

Finally, Michelle stepped back and said to Katie

Lynn, "Actually, I think the whole outfit is hideous . . . just like her mother's singing!"

"Omigosh," Katie Lynn said, rolling her eyes some more. "Don't even get me started on her mother's singing!"

I opened my mouth to say something but no words came out, just a little squeak.

They both laughed.

Michelle grabbed her purse off the counter and said, "Well, at least we won't have to put up with her mother's singing any more after tonight."

"What?" I managed to get out, as they walked around me to the bathroom door.

Michelle paused in the doorway. "Your mother's being *fired* from the church choir tonight."

"Hallelujah!" I heard Katie Lynn say just before the door fell closed and the bathroom fell silent.

Like I said, it turned out that I'd been wrong about a lot of things, but I *had* been right about one thing: it's when other people (or bees) start noticing you that you've really got problems.

I stepped in front of the mirror and yanked the flower out of my hair so hard that tears filled my eyes.

More tears followed, so I locked myself in a stall and sat down on the toilet, folding my legs under me. That way, if someone came into the bathroom, they wouldn't be able to see my feet under the door and hopefully, they'd never know I was there.

I sat on the toilet and thought about what Michelle Snopes had said about Mama. After all, Michelle was the choir director's daughter. If they were really going to fire Mama, she would know. Right?

But after a good while, I decided that it couldn't be true. Now I'll admit that I haven't read the entire Bible, but I still felt pretty sure that Jesus had never said anything like, "Come unto me, all ye that are good singers." I'm pretty sure that Jesus loved everybody, even lepers. (Lepers are people in the Bible who have leprosy, which is a sickness that causes gross, oozing sores all over their skin.) No, Mrs. Snopes couldn't fire Mama even if she'd wanted to, I reasoned, because God wouldn't allow it. And neither would Pastor Cooper.

I took a deep breath. I felt lots better. Okay, I felt a *little* better. Not ready to come out of the bathroom, but better.

I stayed in the bathroom instead of going to Bible study. A few minutes before eight, when choir let out, I decided to go and wait for Mama right outside the choir room door so she wouldn't come looking for me at Bible study.

But on my way to the choir room, I found Mama sitting alone on a bench near the front door in the vestibule (that's the fancy church-word for *lobby*). She looked sad until she saw me coming. Then Mama forced a smile.

I couldn't smile back at her. I was too busy wondering what this meant.

"Choir let out early," Mama said quickly, "so I was just waiting until it was time to come and get you."

"Oh." I nodded.

Mama didn't talk much as we walked home. In fact, she didn't say a word until we reached the drugstore. Then she slowed down. "Let's get a soda," she said.

I relaxed and smiled. Everything was okay. Michelle Snopes was just a big, mean liar.

The bells hanging on the door were still jingling as Mama fished two dollars from her purse and handed it to me. "Go ahead and get whatever you want," she said. "I have to use the restroom."

I nodded, thinking, *ice cream sundae!*

Then Mama said something she had never said to me before: "If there's any change, you can keep it for the quarter machines."

I should've known then, but I didn't. I should've known, because Mama is totally against quarter machines. She calls them junk machines, and always insists that we don't need any more junk. Always, except for tonight. So I should've known something was very wrong. But I didn't because I was too excited about the possibilities. *Soda or ice cream? Gumballs or prizes? Or both?*

Mr. Wheeler balanced his mop against the wall behind the counter, and smiled when he saw me. "Ice cream sundae or cherry cola, Jamie Jo?" he asked.

"Um, how much do those cost?" I said, hoping to

keep as many quarters as possible. *Did Mama say that I absolutely* had *to order something?* I decided that Mama would probably be mad if I spent the whole two dollars on junk machines.

"Cola's a dollar, sundae's a dollar fifty," Mr. Wheeler said.

"Cherry cola," I said. *Yippee! Four quarters left!*

Mr. Wheeler nodded. He handed me my soda and change and went back to mopping. Mama still wasn't back from the bathroom. (To be honest, I thought maybe she was doing number two.)

I slurped down my soda in one mighty gulp and tossed the cup into the trash.

Then, I wandered over to the quarter machines and took my time, trying to make the best decision possible. I crouched and carefully inspected the plastic bubble-wrapped prizes. They all appeared to be the same: silver necklaces with a tear-shaped charm on them that either read: "BE FRI" or "ST ENDS." I knew that those two charms fit together to form a perfect heart that read "BEST FRIENDS." Almost every girl I knew had one of those necklaces. For just a minute, I felt sorry that I didn't have a best friend, but eventually I moved on to purchase four giant gumballs.

I pocketed three gumballs for later. Mama came up behind me just as I was popping a red one into my mouth.

"Well?" she said.

I nodded, tried to smile, and say, "Thank you," but with the giant gumball in my mouth, my smile felt more like a showing of my teeth, like at the dentist's office, and my words sounded more like, "Faunkoooh."

"You're welcome," Mama said.

This time, I tried to smile at Mama with my eyes. That's when I noticed that her face was blotchy and red. She had been crying in the bathroom. My heart sank.

Mama was quiet again as we walked side by side in the warm evening breeze.

Had Michelle been telling the truth? Should I spit out my gumball and ask Mama about choir? What if she started to cry? What if she didn't want to talk about it at all? I didn't want to make Mama cry and I really didn't want to spit out my gumball, either.

I thought and thought as we walked, but I never came up with anything helpful to say. So instead, when my gumball had finally melted into just gum, I said, "Do you think that God loves Michelle Snopes and Katie Lynn Howard?"

"Of course," said Mama. "The Lord loves all of us, Jamie Jo."

I found that hard to believe, and even harder to accept. But I decided that *maybe* God loved Michelle Snopes and Katie Lynn Howard, but if he did, then he *definitely* loved them less. I kept this to myself though, because I didn't want to hear about how God loves Michelle Snopes and Katie Lynn Howard just as much as he loves me, which is what Mama would've said, I know.

We reached the house and started up the front walk. "I think we might give church a rest for a little while, Jamie Jo," Mama said lightly.

That's when I knew. That's when I knew that the earth was somehow shifting beneath our feet, and that things weren't going to be the same. I felt nervous and scared.

I knew that Mama loved Jesus and church and singing like I loved ice cream sundaes and cherry sodas and junk machines, maybe even more.

That night, I begged God to put things right again, to make them the way they always had been.

Chapter Two

By 8:52 on Sunday morning, June 2nd, it was already too hot to sleep, too hot to stay in bed, too hot to get up and move around, just plain *too hot!* I peeled the sheets back off my skin and went downstairs in my nightgown.

As soon as I reached the bottom step, Mama handed me my purple sundress on a hanger. "I washed your favorite dress for church."

I stopped. *Church? Had she forgotten?*

Mama kissed my forehead. "It's Sunday, Jamie Jo," she said, as if I didn't know.

I peered over at Daddy in his big chair, still wearing his pajamas. Without looking up, he said, "You heard your mother. Get dressed."

I sighed loudly. "Okay, but when I come back, can one of you please explain to me again why we don't have air-conditioning?"

"Because it's an old house," Mama said.

"I know," I said, "but we could — "

Daddy lifted his head and shot me a warning look. "Church," he said, like church really mattered to him.

I stomped back upstairs.

Let me tell you, church didn't matter to Daddy one bit. He said he hadn't made his mind up about God yet. It wasn't that he believed there was no God; he just wasn't sure that there *was*. Some days, Daddy told me, he was positive that God was up there, in charge, but other days, things seemed like such a mess, Daddy just couldn't believe that *any*one was in charge of *any*thing. So Daddy never went to church.

Mama said that most people, even Christians, felt this way sometimes, but that Daddy was just more truthful about it.

"I'm leaving in an hour, with or without you," Mama called up to me.

"I know," I said.

Then suddenly, I remembered my prayer, and thought maybe it had been answered. It seemed like things were back to normal!

"Thank you," I said to the cracked ceiling above me.

When I came back downstairs, dressed for church, Mama said, "Where's your purple dress?"

"Oh . . . I, um . . . I just wore that dress to church on Wednesday, Mama."

It was true, but that wouldn't have stopped me before. I loved purple, and I loved that dress. I'd worn it every chance I'd gotten — before I found out that it was "hideous." But now . . . well, now I planned never to wear that dress again.

Mama tilted her head back as if saying to The Lord: *I really don't understand ten-year-old girls these days, do you?*

Mama and I left the house for church at the exact same time as Mrs. Peck, the widow who lived next door. This happened a lot.

"Hello, Mrs. Peck," Mama called out, in her sing-songy way, like she always did.

Mrs. Peck responded in the same way *she* always did. She nodded her head once, then quickly crossed the street.

"I don't understand her," I said to Mama, as we walked across from Mrs. Peck.

"Shhh, lower your voice," Mama said.

"Why doesn't she want to walk with us?" I whispered. "We're coming from the same place, and we're going to the same place, in the same way at the same time!"

"Maybe she's afraid of our flyswatter," Mama said, using it to poke me.

"I'm being serious," I said.

Mama sighed and said, "Oh, Jamie Jo, I'm sure that Mrs. Peck has her reasons."

"Like what?"

"Maybe she's walking for exercise, and she doesn't want to be distracted," Mama suggested.

I looked over at Mrs. Peck. She didn't look like much of an exercise-walker to me. Her grayish dark hair was pulled up into a tight bun on top of her head, and she wore a navy-blue polka dot dress that somehow made her look shorter and rounder than usual. Plus, she had on high heels — *high heels!*

I shook my head. "That's not it."

"How do you know?" Mama said.

"Because I know."

"You don't know, Jamie Jo. You can never know what's going on inside another person's head," Mama said.

"You're right," I said. "What's going on in yours?"

"What do you mean?"

"I mean, why do you keep saying hello to Mrs. Peck when she has never once spoken to you? Is it because she has a swimming pool in her backyard?"

Mama laughed. "No. I speak to her, Jamie Jo, because we are neighbors, and the Bible says that we are supposed to love our neighbors."

"So you love Mrs. Peck by saying hello?"

"I guess so."

"Well, I don't think she loves you back."

"That doesn't matter."

How could it not matter?

"The Bible doesn't say to love the neighbors that

are friendly. The Bible says simply to love your neighbors," Mama added.

I decided that I didn't want to talk anymore. First off, it was too hot outside to talk. And secondly, I didn't want to hear about how God loved Mrs. Peck, just like he loved Michelle Snopes and Katie Lynn Howard.

When we arrived at church, Mama followed me into the sanctuary, and sat down beside me on the pew.

"What are you doing?" I whispered. "Aren't you supposed to go to the choir room?"

"Not today," Mama said.

I hoped this meant that the choir wasn't singing this morning. But a few minutes later the choir spilled into the choir loft.

I looked up at my mother, questioning her with my eyes.

She smiled at me and patted my knee.

I scrunched up my face and aimed my meanest look up into the choir loft, right at Mrs. Peck. So what if she had a swimming pool? I just *knew* it was her fault that Mama had been fired from the choir. She'd never liked Mama, I could tell. Plus, Mrs. Peck was friends with Mrs. Snopes, the choir director, so I figured she had probably poisoned Mrs. Snopes's mind against Mama.

I stared at Mrs. Peck for most of the service. Her face was tight and wrinkled up and disapproving. She wasn't even looking back at me — this was just her natural expression! To be honest, I got tired of looking at Mrs. Peck's face. It didn't make me feel happy to look at it.

So every now and then I allowed my eyes to wander over the faces of all thirteen choir members. I missed seeing Mama's face among them. When Mama was in the choir loft, her eyes sparkled and she smiled *the whole time!* And when she sang . . . well, she made singing look like the best, happiest, most fun thing a person could do!

I barely heard a word that Pastor Cooper said that morning. I know he went on for more than an hour, because my watch told me so and because I got *really* hungry. But the only thing I heard him say was, "There is purpose in all things."

And anyhow, I didn't believe it. I didn't believe it any more than I believed that Mrs. Peck exercise-walked to church in her high heels.

"Why can't we just go to a different church?" I asked Mama as we were walking back home.

"Why would we do that?"

I was silent for a minute, thinking. Finally, I said quietly, "Because they fired you from the choir, Mama."

Mama stopped walking, her eyes wide. "They didn't fire me. You can't be fired from church choir!"

"Then how come you didn't sing today?"

"I decided not to audition," Mama said, holding her head as high as a queen, the flyswatter like a scepter in her hand.

"Audition?"

"Yes," Mama said. "It was decided that from now on, there will be auditions for the church choir. Last Wednesday night, they auditioned everybody."

I remembered Mama sitting on the bench in the vestibule. "But you didn't try out?"

"No, I didn't. I'm not a good singer, Jamie Jo. We all know that."

"Were you scared?" I asked, even as I told myself that *that* couldn't be it, because Mama wasn't even scared of bees!

"No, I wasn't scared, Jamie Jo. I was just honest with myself. I know I'm not a good singer," Mama said. Then she took my hand and started walking again.

"But you love to sing," I said, "and you could be in the choir at some other church."

"Church is like home, Jamie Jo, and the people there are like family. You don't up and leave your home and your family just because of a little disagreement," Mama said.

"So you *do* disagree," I said, just to be sure. "I mean, with the audition thing."

"I was hurt at first," Mama admitted, "and I thought about taking a few weeks off from church, just to let the hurt heal a little. But even so, I can't really say that I disagree."

"Why not?" I was totally confused.

Mama thought about it. "Because I don't know yet," she finally said. "I'll just have to see where it leads. Like Pastor Cooper said, 'There is purpose in all things,' even this, Jamie Jo."

I didn't buy it. I felt like shouting at the sky, *Hey, are you up there? Are you paying attention?* I supposed this was how Daddy felt sometimes.

We stopped on the corner before crossing the street to wait for a car to pass. When it did, Michelle Snopes's face appeared in the rear window. She was sticking her tongue out at me! (Of course, Mama didn't notice.)

I told myself that this was awfully childish behavior for a twelve-year-old, which Michelle Snopes was. But it still bothered me.

Actually, it felt like everything was bothering me lately: Katie Lynn Howard, Michelle Snopes, Mrs. Snopes and the audition business, Mrs. Peck, my growling stomach, the suffocating heat, and the fact that we didn't have air-conditioning — or a dog.

When we arrived home, I announced my biggest complaint at that moment: "I'm starving!"

"You can have an apple while I make lunch," Mama offered.

It wasn't an ice cream sundae, but I figured an apple was better than nothing.

We found Daddy sitting at the kitchen table, having traded his book for the Sunday newspaper.

"Pate's home," he said, lowering the paper so that we could just see his eyes.

I thought this was good news, because even though my brother had grown up and left the house a long time ago, I still missed him something awful.

Mama must've thought that this was good news too, because she said, "Wonderful," as she took her apron off the hook.

"He brought his suitcase with him," Daddy said, raising one eyebrow to give Mama a meaningful look.

"Probably his laundry," Mama said. She pretended not to notice Daddy's look.

"Too bad all of Pate's clothes aren't the same like yours are, Daddy," I said. "If they were, then Pate could wear the same old dirty clothes over and over and nobody would ever know!" (Daddy's shirts are all white, his suits are all black, and even though his ties are different, they're all red.)

Daddy gave me a disgusted look.

For some reason, the room felt heavy, like a dark rain cloud about to burst. Daddy seemed irritable, and on his way to angry. Mama pretended not to notice Daddy's mood, but she worked so hard at pretending, that I knew she'd noticed, all right. Still, I followed Mama's lead, and pretended everything was fine.

I grabbed an apple out of the basket on the table and started twisting the stem. "A . . . B . . . C . . . D . . ." The stem broke off on D. "I'm going to marry someone whose name starts with the letter D."

"Doctor," Daddy said right away. "That's good. Marry a doctor, Jamie Jo. We need a doctor in the family."

I nodded. This wasn't the first time that Daddy had told me to marry a doctor.

Mama put a hand on her hip. "She doesn't have to *marry* a doctor; Jamie Jo can *be* a doctor if she wants to."

Just then, we heard the washing machine start up in the basement.

Mama gave Daddy her best *I-told-you-so* look. I know, because I get that one a lot. But she was too late. Daddy had already buried his face in the newspaper again.

Pate didn't come upstairs until Mama called, "Lunch!"

He shouldn't have bothered even then, because it turned out that lunch was tuna casserole. Ick!

But then again, Mama had always said, "Pate'll eat anything that isn't nailed down."

It must've been true, because Pate piled tuna casserole onto his plate like he hadn't seen food in a week.

I hoped that the dish would be empty by the time it was passed to me. To be honest, I was a little iffy about tuna fish to begin with. Meat from a can just didn't seem right to me, and I drew the line at *warm* tuna fish.

But when Mama handed me the dish, it wasn't even close to being empty. *If only I had a dog to sneak food to under the table,* I thought for the millionth time.

The very second that everyone's plates were loaded, before Mama could even say grace, Daddy said, "So Pate, what's Vicky up to today that she couldn't join us?"

Vicky was my brother's wife. *His second wife — in only two and a half years,* Daddy pointed out at every chance he got.

The room suddenly felt heavy again, only this time, even heavi*er.* I expected a clap of thunder any second.

Pate dropped his fork. Mama gave Daddy a look. Daddy stared at Pate, waiting for an answer, and I stared at my plate like I was fascinated by tuna casserole.

"Uh . . . well," Pate took a deep breath before continuing. "Uh . . . Vicky and I . . . well, we're having a little trouble."

Daddy leaned forward. "Is this because you don't have a job?"

"I have a job," Pate insisted.

Daddy leaned back against his chair and folded his arms over his chest. "Planting flowers in other people's gardens in the spring and summer isn't a real job any more than teaching kids to play the guitar in the fall and winter is a real job."

"Landscaping is a real job, just like teaching is a real job," Pate said. "Which one is it that bothers you?"

Daddy stood up. "It *all* bothers me, Pate," he thundered. Then he left the table.

Pate hung his head. Mama covered Pate's hand with hers and said softly, "Don't worry. I'll talk to him."

"May I be excused?" I said. If I was going to get out of eating tuna casserole, now was the time.

Mama didn't even look at my plate. Instead she just said, "You may."

I skedaddled out of the kitchen before Mama had time to recognize her mistake.

When I got to my room, I turned the fan on full blast and flung myself onto the bed. I felt bad for Pate. I heard Daddy again in my mind: "It *all* bothers me, Pate."

It was the way he'd said the word *all* that somehow let me know that Daddy was going back a long time.

35

If you ask me, grown-ups remember way too much. For example, every Thursday night during the school year, Daddy asks me, "Have you studied for your spelling test tomorrow?" He does this because *once,* when I was in first grade — *first grade!* — I'd forgotten to study and had gotten a "C" on my spelling test. So, for the past four years, I'd answered the same question, the same question that I was doomed to answer every Thursday night for the rest of my life. Does this seem fair to you?

Mama slipped into my room then, and closed the door behind her. When I saw the ice cream sundae in her hand, I realized that Mama knew exactly how much tuna casserole I'd eaten (or *not* eaten) and she was desperate to get more food into me.

I am the kind of skinny that causes my tights to bag and wrinkle around my knees and ankles in the wintertime, the kind of skinny that makes me look like all arm bones and leg bones in the summertime, the kind of skinny that makes other mothers say to my mother, "Feed that child, Libby!"

Mama *tried* to feed me, but I didn't make it easy,

which is why Daddy sometimes calls me Princess Picky, and not in a good way. Anyhow, when Mama really got desperate, she went straight for the ice cream sundaes.

"Thank you, Mama," I said.

She nodded and sat down on my bed.

"Did you talk to Daddy?" I asked in between bites.

Mama sighed. "Not yet."

"I don't understand why he's so mad at Pate."

Mama thought about this for a while. I was almost finished with my sundae by the time she answered. "I think the problem is that Pate's more like me, and Daddy hoped that Pate would be more like him."

"How come?" I said. After all, Mama was a good person, a great person, I thought.

"Daddy hoped that Pate would finish college, and go to work at a job, one job, where he would wear a suit and tie every day. And that he would get married, one time, and have a family . . . and generally live his life more like Daddy did."

"Does Pate know that?"

Mama smiled. "I'm sure he does, Jamie Jo."

"Then how come he didn't do what Daddy wanted?" After all, you're supposed to do what your parents want, right?

"Pate has to live his own life in his own way," Mama said.

That sounded about right to me.

Chapter Three

The heat woke me up at 7:44 on Monday, June 3rd, which was a good thing. Otherwise, I might've missed the moving van that pulled into the driveway across the street right after breakfast.

I sat down on the window seat in the front room and watched.

The first person out of the van was a girl about my age. She had curly, dark-brown hair, and purple high-top tennis shoes. Carefully, she lifted a cardboard box out of the van, and then a big black dog (a dog!) jumped out of the van. The dog was very interested in whatever the girl had in the box, but I couldn't tell what that might be from my perch in the front window.

Then the girl disappeared inside the house for a few minutes, but soon she came running back outside, smiling and laughing, playing around with her parents. Her dad messed her hair and the girl laughed. Her mom tickled her under her arm as she reached for something inside the van. The girl spun around laughing some more. They all seemed happy and nice.

Suddenly, I found myself hoping that the curly-headed girl and I would be friends. She looked like the kind of girl that I would be friends with, if I were the kind of the girl that made friends. But I didn't really have too many friends. Friends tend to notice you, and I didn't like to be noticed. I liked to blend in and be very quiet. And I liked to *hope* that no one would ask me to go anywhere or do anything outside (without my mother and the flyswatter, that is).

But of course, people did. For example, when school started last year, Miss Tucker asked me to come outside with the rest of my class for recess. I said, "No, thank you." (Also, I held onto my desk, tight.) I was very nice about the whole thing, very polite — honest I was! But still, Miss Tucker called my mama on me! After that day, I *had* to go outside for recess (both Mama *and* Miss Tucker said so). But I didn't play, and I didn't really make friends with anybody, except for Miss Tucker. During recess, she let me sit on the teachers' bench, where I huddled close to her, hugging my backpack (because my fly-swatter was hidden in there) and looked out for bees!

This sounds bad, I know. I knew it even then, but I also knew I wasn't the only person that ever felt this way. My cousin, Mary Louise, never went anywhere either, because she sucked her thumb constantly and did this weird twirly thing with her hair, and she didn't want anyone to know about it. So what if Mary Louise was only seven years old and I was ten?

Oh sure, our families had tried to encourage Mary Louise and me, the thumb-sucker/hair twirler and the bee-phobic, to be friends. But it turned out that, aside from being a little different and wanting to stay home, Mary Louise and I didn't have that much in common. Plus, Mary Louise was *really* whiny. Every time she talked, I found myself wishing that she'd put her thumb back in her mouth.

Anyway, now the curly-headed girl across the street was holding a basketball and talking to her dad. He shook his head, and she looked disappointed. Then, he smacked the ball out of her hands and took off dribbling down the driveway. The girl laughed.

"Are you going to sit there staring all day, Jamie Jo, or are you going to go over there and introduce yourself?" Mama said, coming up behind me.

I turned. "Will you come with me?" I asked in a small voice.

"How about I watch you from the front window?" Mama said.

I shook my head.

"Oh, Jamie Jo, they're just right across the street."

I turned back around, to look out the window, rather than at Mama's face, as I shook my head again. I knew she was disappointed. I didn't need to *see* it.

I watched the family across the street unload their furniture. It was easy to pick out the stuff that belonged to the girl, because it was all really brightly colored compared to everything else in the moving truck.

"Watcha doin', Squirt?" Pate said, when he came upstairs.

"New neighbors," I said, pointing out the window. "Want to go over there with me?"

Pate shrugged. "Maybe later."

"When?"

"When I get back. I gotta go over to the Garrett place and plant some holly hocks. They're being delivered right now."

"What are holly hocks?" I asked.

"Big, showy flowers."

"Oh," I said.

Pate started to walk away.

"Pate?" I said.

"Yeah?"

"When we go across the street, will you carry Mama's flyswatter?"

Pate stopped and turned around. "Aw, come on, Jamie Jo. You mean to tell me you're *still* not over that bee thing?"

I turned my back on him. I didn't feel like talking anymore.

But Pate didn't get the message. He said, "Did you know that without bees our food crops wouldn't be pollinated?"

"So what?" I said, watching Pate's reflection in the glass.

"So, we wouldn't have any food, Jamie Jo, and without food, we'd die. All of us. People can't survive without bees. Bees are good."

I really wanted to have the last word, but by the time I thought of something to say back, I saw Pate through the window. He turned out of our driveway and zipped down the street on his motorbike, his gardening tools strapped to his back.

I got up and went to stand behind the screen door, trying to judge the exact distance between our house and the house across the street. I estimated that it would take me five steps to cross the front porch. *Five steps, then six stairs . . .*

I stepped out onto the porch and studied the front walk. It was too long. I wouldn't be able to get back inside the house fast enough if I encountered a bee. And even if I could make it that far, I still had the street to cross! Nope, the house across the street was just too far to go without Mama and the flyswatter.

I hurried back inside to wait.

I waited on the window seat almost all morning, but no one ever came and offered to walk me across the street — not even Pate.

That night at dinner, Pate said, "Guess what, Squirt?"

"Mmmm?" I said, my mouth full of corn on the cob.

"I got stung by a bee today."

My eyes bulged.

Pate nodded. "Yeah, and it really wasn't that bad . . ."

I didn't believe him. And I didn't plan on stepping foot outside the house without Mama ever again. After all, Pate had gone out without her, and he'd been attacked by a bee! I shuddered at the thought.

Mama watched me for a minute. Then she sighed

sadly, and said under her breath, "I wish we'd never watched that movie."

"What movie?" Pate said.

I knew what movie. On a blaring hot Monday last summer, while I was still in the *burn* phase of my *freckle, burn, peel* sunning process, Mama and I had stayed in and watched the movie *My Girl.* In it, there was a very sensitive boy named Thomas (who looked to me like he might freckle, burn, and peel, too) and he had *died* of bee stings! Naturally, I'd cried my eyes out over poor Thomas! After the movie was over, I'd turned to Mama and said, "Could that really happen?" Mama had said, "I suppose so." And that was it. Right then and there, I'd silently vowed never to go back outside alone ever, ever again.

"What movie?" Pate said again. "You're not sayin' Jamie Jo's afraid of bees because of some silly *movie,* are you?"

Mama shook her head at Pate, just barely. That meant one of two things: *Stop it* or *Drop it.* In this case, it meant for Pate to drop the subject of bees.

And just what was Pate doing bringing up the sore

subject of bees anyway? After all, I never brought up subjects that might be sore for him! I never said anything like, *I really miss Vicky.* Or Sandy, Pate's first wife. Not that I missed either one of them.

I gave Pate my *I'm-mad-at-you* look across the table.

But he ignored me. "Mama, the nursery's gonna deliver some plants and flowers and things for you on Saturday. To thank me for all the business I've been giving them."

"Thank you, son," Mama said.

Pate nodded, as he sopped up gravy with his biscuit. "You just decide where you want everything, and I'll do the plantin' Sunday morning while you're at church, before it gets too hot."

Mama looked at Daddy like, *See? See what a good boy we have?*

Daddy never looked up from his chicken and dumplings. He loves chicken and dumplings. In fact, he never said a word until his plate was clean.

Then Daddy laid his napkin on the table and said

to Pate, "I appreciate you helping your mother while you're here."

I knew what Daddy was really saying. He meant: You *will* help your mother while you're here.

Pate nodded, and seemed grateful.

I was grateful, too. Grateful that Daddy hadn't done The Job Report, which is what he usually did over dinner when Pate was home. The Job Report is when Daddy tells Pate about all the jobs all over town that he thinks Pate should apply for.

Pate pushed back from the table. "Hey, Squirt, wanna come downstairs for a jam session?"

He must've known that I was mad at him after all. And I really was. But that is not a good reason to miss a jam session. (A jam session is when Pate plays his guitar and we sing together like rock stars.)

I sat down on Pate's bed while he picked up his guitar and began tuning.

"Did you know that Daddy wants you to wear a suit and tie to work?" I asked him.

Pate looked up from his guitar and smiled a sad

smile. "Well, maybe you can wear the suit for him when you grow up."

"He doesn't want me to wear a suit," I said. "He wants me to marry a doctor."

Pate rolled his eyes, and said, "Are we singing here or what?"

"We're singing," I said.

Chapter Four

The next day, a day that I remember as Temptation Tuesday, I went back to watching the house across the street from my place in the front window.

The curly-headed girl started out roller-skating around her house, up and down the front walk, around in circles on the driveway, and back and forth on the street. I loved roller skating, *inside,* at the roller skating rink.

For a while, I tried waving to the girl from the window. I thought maybe I could get her to come over to *my* house, but I never could get her attention.

After that, the girl played some basketball in her driveway. It looked like fun, but it made me feel even more miserable. It looked like so much fun that I moved from the front window to the front door. I thought that maybe the glass was the problem, that maybe there was some sort of glare, making it impossible for her to see me. So, I stood behind the screen door and waved some more. No luck.

At 11:27, a white van pulled into the driveway across the street. On the side, the van read: *Franklin Heating and Cooling.* Was it possible that the new neighbors were putting air-conditioning in the house? *Oh, to have air-conditioning!*

This was the thought that caused me to open the screen door, and step out onto the front porch — without Mama and her flyswatter.

I saw myself happily dashing across the street to cool off, no Mama, no flyswatter, just me. And that's how I knew I was daydreaming.

When I blinked my eyes, I was still standing on our front porch, only now I spotted a huge bumble bee in the front yard! I backed slowly toward the door, and slipped inside the house. *Whew! That was close!*

But by the time I returned to window seat, I felt like I'd lost something. What? I had no idea.

After lunch, I said to Mama, "You aren't doing a very good job of loving our neighbors across the street."

"I see," Mama said, opening the refrigerator. She pulled out a beautiful strawberry pie and said, "Well, then I guess I'd better take this pie over there."

I shot out of my chair, down the hall, and up the stairs, hollering, "I just have to get my shoes. Don't leave without me!"

Mama was waiting for me at the front door when I came back down.

"Where's the flyswatter?" I asked.

"We don't need it, you'll see," Mama said calmly. "We're just going across the street."

"We *need* it," I pleaded. "I saw a big, humongo bumble bee in our front yard this morning."

Mama pressed her lips together tightly and pulled the lime-green flyswatter out of the umbrella stand in our front hall. "Open the door for me."

"Wait," I said.

"Yes?"

"If they ask about the flyswatter, I think you

should tell them that you didn't want any bugs to get in the pie," I said.

Mama's eyes widened and she stared at me. "I'm not going to lie," she said. "And for future reference, when you feel the need to lie about your behavior, then it's time to change your behavior."

"But — " I started.

"Just open the door, Jamie Jo."

It was exactly forty-one steps from our front door to the front door across the street. I counted. Thank goodness I'd brought Mama and the flyswatter, because forty-one steps was a lot.

The black dog and the curly-headed girl met us at the front door, her mother coming up behind them. It turned out that their last name was Yell. How cool is that?

Mama and Mrs. Yell talked for a few minutes on the front porch, and then Mrs. Yell introduced her daughter, Rafael (Rafi for short), who was ten.

"I like your name . . . and your shoes," I said. "And also your dog."

"Thanks," Rafi said. "Her name's Crooner. You can pet her if you want."

I knelt and petted Crooner until she made this low, gurgly, growly sound.

I withdrew my hands then, and looked up at Rafi.

"Oh, she's just talking to you," Rafi said. "She likes to talk. And sing."

"Are you sure?" I said.

"Yeah," Rafi said. "Hey! Wanna come upstairs and see my room?"

I peered over at Mama. She was still talking to Mrs. Yell, but she was wrapping up, about to say good-bye, I could tell.

"No thanks," I said. Besides, I already had a pretty good idea of what Rafi's room looked like: dark purple chest of drawers, light purple nightstands, double bed with a green headboard.

Rafi's cheeks turned pink and she studied her purple tennis shoes.

I'd hurt her feelings, I realized. I kind of wanted to tell Rafi about the bee thing then, but I couldn't. I just couldn't.

Exactly forty-one steps later, I was back to my window seat.

At 3:38, the Franklin Heating and Cooling van backed out of the Yells' driveway.

At 4:05, Rafi appeared. She unfolded a yellow lawn chair, set it up at the end of their driveway, and went back into her house.

At 4:11, Rafi came back out, carrying the mysterious cardboard box that I'd seen the day before. Crooner followed along excitedly. Rafi sat down in the lawn chair, and turned the box in her lap, until I could read the front. It said FREE PUPPIES in bold, dripping red letters.

My heart skipped a beat and then tried to leap out of my chest!

That night at dinner, I began The Canine Campaign. I begged my parents for a dog, with points and reasons. *Good* reasons!

"No," Mama said to me, passing the mashed potatoes to Daddy.

"Hat," Daddy said to Pate, spooning potatoes onto his plate.

Pate removed his baseball hat and tossed it onto the floor.

Daddy shook his head and sighed.

I gave Pate a look that said, *Hey, you're not helping me here!*

But Pate was distracted by all the food.

"Dogs stink," Daddy said then.

What kind of a person would say such a thing? I wondered.

"Dogs don't stink!" I shot back. "Dogs are great. *Everybody* likes dogs!"

"No," Daddy said. "I'm saying they actually smell bad, Jamie Jo."

"Oh . . . well, ours won't, because I'll give him a bath . . . every day."

"No," Daddy said, reaching for the salt and pepper.

"But a dog would be so much fun!" I continued. "Plus he could protect us, Daddy." Daddy was big on safety and protection.

"No," Daddy said again.

I gave up on Daddy then, and instead said to

Mama, "You'd never have to throw leftovers away again. Our dog could eat them!" Mama hated to throw food away.

"No," Mama said softly.

I balled my hands into little fists in frustration, and blurted, "I have to live my own life, in my own way!" (I knew that little tidbit would come in handy.)

Pate laughed out loud.

Mama covered her mouth with her napkin, but I could tell by her eyes that she was smiling and trying not to laugh.

Daddy gave Mama a look. He was not smiling.

Mama replaced her napkin in her lap, cleared her throat, and said, "Jamie Jo, you are not ready to care for a dog."

"You always say that," I said, "but I *am* ready! I have everything a dog needs: a collar, a leash, dishes, and a bed! I even read the whole book about how to train dogs!"

"That isn't what we mean when we say you aren't ready," Daddy said.

This was news to me, news that I wished they'd

shared *before* I'd spent every penny in my piggy bank getting ready for a dog.

"What do you mean then?" I said.

"Dogs have to be trained," Daddy said.

"I know," I said quickly. "I'll do it."

"Potty trained," Mama said, *"outside."*

This slowed me down. *Bees* live outside.

Daddy set his fork down on his plate. "So," he said, "who's going to take this pup outside a hundred times a day to go to the bathroom?"

I shrank in my chair, and peered over at Pate.

Pate looked like he felt bad for me, but he didn't offer to help. He just stuffed more mashed potatoes and gravy into his mouth. Some big brother he was!

Then the strangest thing happened. I heard myself say, "I will. I'll take the puppy outside."

"By yourself?" Mama said, like she didn't believe me.

"Uh-huh," I managed to say, in a small voice, even though my stomach was doing somersaults.

"Jamie Jo, do you mean to tell me that after a whole year of refusing to leave the house without your mother and the flyswatter, now, all of a sudden, you're willing to go outside all by yourself? Just like that?" Daddy said.

"Weeeell," I said, my voice sounding screechy in my own ears. "I won't exactly be by myself, right? I mean, I'll have a puppy with me, right?"

Mama smiled and looked at Daddy hopefully.

Daddy's eyes rolled upward toward the ceiling and stayed there, which meant that he was thinking. Finally he said, "Tell you what, Jamie Jo. You go across the street bright and early tomorrow and ask if you can *borrow* a puppy, just for the day. You take care of that puppy all by yourself, all day long, including taking it outside, all by yourself. And if you still want the pup at the end of the day, then I'll consider it."

I nodded my head. I felt too sick to open my mouth. I was afraid something other than words might come out. *Do we really need a dog? After all, dogs do stink.*

I was the only one still sitting at the table, holding onto my chair with both hands, when Mama began clearing the dishes.

"You okay, Jamie Jo?" she asked, turning on the faucet.

I gripped my chair so hard it hurt my hands. "Fine," I squeaked.

Mama nodded. Then she reached over, turned on the radio, and began to sing along.

It wasn't good singing, but still, it made me feel a little better. I felt well enough to move from my chair to my bed upstairs, where I fell asleep holding my stomach.

Chapter Five

It was still dark when I got out of bed on Wednesday morning, June 5th. But by then, I'd boiled my problem down to this: did I love dogs more than I hated bees? *Yes,* I told myself.

I dressed quickly, picked up my sandals, and tiptoed downstairs, where I took my place at the front window. As soon as I saw a light go on in the house across the street, I planned to march right over there and get my dog. *My* dog!

A downstairs window lit up in the Yell house at 6:09. *Great! Time to go!*

At 9:02 I still hadn't made it across the street, but I hadn't given up. Okay, so I'd given up about fifty-six times, but I hadn't given up *completely.*

The first time I'd stepped out onto the front porch, I'd almost made it to the stairs. But then I'd gotten scared and rushed back inside. This happened about twenty times.

Then I began to realize the problem with giving up. When you give up, it really just means that you have to start over. After all, I'd crossed the five steps on my front porch twenty times! That's a hundred steps, and Rafi's house was only forty-one steps away! If I hadn't given up and turned back, I could've made it to Rafi's house in forty-one steps, and back home in another forty-one steps, and I still I would've taken only eighty-two steps! But no, I'd taken a hundred steps *and* I was still right here on my own front porch — without a dog! See what I mean?

That's when I got serious. I stepped out onto the front porch again, and immediately spotted that same humongo bee in our front yard. My legs got wobbly, but I refused to give up. So I slid down the screen door onto my behind, like a cartoon character, and sat there waiting to catch my breath. As soon as I could breathe a little better, I moved forward on my behind. *Scooch. Scooch.* But Humongo had a friend, so I shifted backward on my behind. *Sliiiiide.* This seemed to go on forever. *Scooch, scooch . . . sliiiide. Scooch, scooch . . . sliiiide.*

I admit it wasn't a pretty sight, certainly not the brave and glorious victory I'd imagined at 6:09 this morning. But somehow it landed me on the Yells' front porch at 9:38.

I knocked fast.

Rafi answered the door.

"Um, hey," I said. "I was just wondering if you had any puppies left . . . and um, could I come in?"

"Sure," Rafi said, stepping back.

Safe! I thought when Rafi closed the front door behind me.

"The puppies are out in the backyard," Rafi said. "Follow me."

"Um, could I have a drink of water first?" I asked. "Inside?"

I sat down at the kitchen table while Rafi poured me a tall glass of ice water.

"My dad said to ask you if I could just *borrow* a puppy, for today," I said.

Rafi looked confused as she handed me the glass and sat down. "Borrow?"

"Yeah, see, Daddy wants me to have a better understanding of the responsibility I'm taking on with a puppy."

I thought that sounded pretty good, very parental, especially the *better understanding* and *responsibility* parts.

"And then what?" Rafi said.

"And then if I still want a puppy, after I have this better understanding and all, then I can probably have it."

"That'd be great," Rafi said. "I wanted to keep one of the puppies, but my parents said no."

I nodded. *Wow. That was so easy.* I hadn't had to explain my freakish bee phobia or anything!

"But if one of the puppies lived across the street, then I'd still get to see it, right?" Rafi said.

"Right, anytime you want," I said, relaxing a little and looking around. There was an air-conditioner sticking through the kitchen window, just like the one at my house.

"That'd be great," Rafi said again.

"Yeah," I said. "So, are y'all getting air-conditioning in the *whole house?*"

"No," Rafi said. "I thought we were going to, but this morning my dad said it would cost too much, and that we shouldn't rip up this old house like that."

I smiled. "My dad says that, too." Then I lowered my voice and did my best imitation of Daddy: "Jamie Jo, it'd be a real shame to have to compromise the integrity of a beautiful old house like this. Yessiree, a real shame."

Rafi giggled.

"Do you have a window air-conditioner in your room?" I asked.

"No, just a fan," Rafi said. She didn't sound too happy about her fan.

"Me, too. Just a fan," I said, only I *was* happy. Not about my fan, but about the fact that I might, maybe, possibly be in the process of making a friend.

I drank every drop of water from my glass, s-l-o-wl-y, trying to put off going back outside for as long as possible. Then I shook the ice in my glass, hoping Rafi would offer me more water.

She didn't. Instead, she got up and said, "Let's go choose your puppy!"

I hesitated at the back door, but then followed Rafi out into the backyard. After all, I'd been outside (mostly) for more than three hours, and so far I hadn't been stung by any bees. Plus, I hadn't come this far only to die of embarrassment, after I'd survived crossing the street. And I *would've* died if I'd had to explain my whole bee thing to Rafi! (And yes, this time, I mean *die* in the dramatic *oh-I-would-just-die-if-that-happened-to-me* way.)

There were five puppies in the grass. They were mostly black, like Crooner, but each puppy had some white spots, speckles, or markings. None of them looked like they'd grown into their skins yet. They all had loose, floppy puppy faces, and they were just about the cutest things I'd ever seen. Three of the puppies were playing with each other, and two were sleeping side by side in a sunny spot on the lawn.

Crooner immediately came over to check us out, but she must've decided that we were okay, because after she sniffed us, she stretched out in the grass.

Rafi and I played with the puppies, petted them, and held them. And do you know what? I had such a good time that I forgot to be afraid, for a little while at least.

"So which one do you like?" Rafi said, getting to her feet and wiping her hands on her shorts.

I stood, too, and scratched at the itchy rash the grass had made on the backs of my legs. Then I let my eyes wander over all of the puppies, until they came to rest on the one that was licking my toes at that moment.

"Oh, you don't want that one," Rafi said when she looked over at me.

"Why not?" I asked.

"That one's the runt," Rafi said.

"He's not a runt," I said, because there was no need for name-calling. After all, just because this puppy was a little smaller, that was no good reason to haul off and call him something ugly, like *runt*.

"Yes he is," Rafi said certainly. "He's the smallest of the litter, and the smallest is called The Runt."

I squatted and petted The Runt protectively.

"And my dad says he's not right in the head," Rafi added.

"Just because he's the smallest?" I said. "That's not fair."

"No, not because he's the smallest," Rafi said. "Because he's not right in the head."

I kept petting, only now I cooed to the puppy, too, the way grown-ups sometimes coo to babies. "You're a good boy, aren't you? Yes, you are. You're a good boy," I assured him.

Then I spotted the bee. It was buzzing around a patch of violets in the grass, about a foot away from me.

I froze.

The bee came closer. *Bzzzzzzz!*

The Runt stopped licking my toes and lifted his head to listen.

Spots appeared in front of my eyes. I blinked. More spots.

"Jamie Jo?" Rafi said. She sounded far away, even

though I could see that she was still standing right beside me.

I opened my mouth to scream, but before I could, The Runt leapt into the air, caught the bee in his mouth, chewed, and swallowed.

I stared at him.

The Runt seemed okay — good, even. He was wagging his tail and looking up at me like, *Hey, that was delicious! Got any more of those?*

"See?" Rafi said. "I told you, he's not right in the head."

Since I hadn't felt right in the head all day *(scooch, scooch, slide)* and since The Runt had saved my life and all, I said, "I'll take him."

Rafi shook her head like she had serious doubts about my decision-making abilities. "Okay," she said, "if you're sure."

"I'm sure," I said. "Can I take him home now?"

I did better getting back home. After all, I'd made it across the street once already, which meant there was at least a chance that I could do it again. And this time I wasn't alone. I figured that my chances of making it had been greatly improved by my friend, the bee-eating runt. Plus, I *had* to do better this time. I was pretty sure that Rafi was watching us go, and I still didn't want her to know about my freakish fear of bees. I definitely didn't want her to see me do the *scooch-scooch-slide.* Plus, I was going to need a bathroom soon. I'd drunk a lot of water at Rafi's.

On top of all that, I was hungry. I'd worked up an appetite, what with all that pacing back and forth across the front porch, the scooching and the sliding, and then of course, my brush with death in Rafi's backyard.

When I arrived safely in our kitchen, carrying the puppy, Mama squealed with delight and held out her hands. She must've secretly wanted a puppy too!

"Oh, Jamie Jo! He's so cute!" Mama said, cuddling the puppy in her arms.

"I know! Look at the little ring of white around his eye!"

Mama turned him around to look. "Oh, for goodness sake, if that's not the cutest! And look, he has a little cowlick on top of his head!"

I hadn't noticed it, but he did, and it made me giggle. "He has a puppy-mohawk," I said.

After I made a quick trip to the bathroom, Mama fixed The Runt and me a bacon and egg sandwich.

I ate first, following the pack rules that dogs live by, so that The Runt would know that I was The Boss. (My book said that to train a dog, you had to first understand pack rules.)

Then I tore the remainder of my sandwich into little pieces and fed them to the puppy.

The Runt gulped them down without chewing.

I stared at him and hoped he wasn't choking in some silent, unseen way.

The Runt blinked at me.

Well, if the bee didn't hurt him, I told myself, *this probably won't either.*

When we finished our lunch, Mama said, "Take the puppy outside now, Jamie Jo. It's important that you always take him out right after he eats."

I stood, turned around, and said, "Look at this terrible rash on the backs of my legs!" I scratched at it.

"I think you'll live," Mama said gently.

I picked up the puppy (and the flyswatter) and headed for the front door.

"Why don't you take him out back, away from the street?" Mama called after me.

"Too many flowers, too many bees," I said.

After all, just because The Runt had swallowed one bee didn't mean that he would swallow *all* bees. And really, how many times could a ten-year-old girl expect a seven-week-old puppy to save her life in one day?

I told the heroic bee-eating story that night at dinner. I'm not sure my family believed me, but why would I make a thing like that up?

"So," Daddy said, "have you decided on a name for him?"

That's when I knew that we were keeping the puppy. I smiled at Daddy. He smiled back.

"How about Bee Slayer," I said enthusiastically, "and we can call him B.S. for short!"

Pate laughed so hard he almost fell out of his chair. I had no idea what was so funny.

I looked at Mama for an explanation, but she just said, "I think not."

"Absolutely not," Daddy said.

I felt like maybe I was in trouble, even though I wasn't sure why.

After that, the table was quiet while everyone tried to think of a name.

"What about Buzz?" I said, in almost a whisper.

Everyone nodded and agreed.

"Hello, Buzz," I said to the puppy at my feet.

As soon as he heard the "zz" part of his name, Buzz cocked his head to the side, and stared at me intently, like, *Hey, do you have a bee in your mouth?*

It was quiet on our street when I took Buzz out to use the bathroom at 8:18 that evening. It was so quiet that I could hear the phone ringing inside our house from the front yard.

I was getting impatient. Buzz sniffed every square inch of our front yard, including the mailbox, and then — finally! — did his business.

"Good boy," I gushed. "Good boy! Let's go get you a treat for being such a good boy!"

But Buzz and I both forgot about the treat when we walked into the kitchen. Mama and Daddy were standing by the phone hugging each other. Mama was crying softly into Daddy's shoulder.

I put Buzz down on the floor and he scampered over to Mama's feet, whimpering and fretting.

"What happened?" I said.

Mama didn't answer. She just cried harder.

Daddy turned to me and said in a low voice, "Pastor Cooper just called, Jamie Jo." Then he shook his head once, like he couldn't believe what he was about to tell me.

I waited.

"The church," Daddy said. "There was an explosion tonight, about ten minutes after choir practice was supposed to start. There's nothing left. The whole building, everything, is just . . . *gone.*"

I felt a lump in my throat. I began to tremble all over. Then I burst into tears.

Buzz hurried over to me, sat down at my feet, and began to howl. The low, mournful sound only made me cry harder.

Then Michelle Snopes and Katie Lynn Howard popped into my head, and I knew that I'd been right.

God really did love me more, because after all, I hadn't been at church tonight because Mama wasn't in the choir anymore. *But Michelle and Katie Lynn . . .* I started to sob uncontrollably for the girls that hated me, for the girls I thought that I had hated back, for Mrs. Snopes, and even for Mrs. Peck. None of them deserved *this. This* was awful, worse than awful.

And then I thought of everybody else in the church choir, and their kids who were in my Bible study class, and Miss Noel, our teacher. I wasn't so sure then that God loved me more, because suddenly I wasn't so sure that God existed. I mean, if he was up there, wouldn't he have protected his church, his people? This just didn't make any sense to me.

I cried so hard that my whole body shook. I cried because I suddenly knew that Daddy was right. God wasn't up there, watching over us, after all, and I had *really* hoped that he was. I cried so hard I thought I might throw up.

I cried until Mama knelt in front of me, and took both of my hands in hers. "You don't understand, Jamie Jo."

I tried to quiet myself some then so that I could hear her. Buzz quieted, too. He went from howling back to whimpering.

"There was no one in the church," Mama said. "Everyone in the choir, everyone in your Bible study class, even Mrs. Snopes and Miss Noel — everyone was running late tonight."

I hiccupped.

"No one was there," Mama said again, louder, stronger, more certain.

I nodded my understanding, and felt relief spreading through me. I took a deep breath and blinked my eyes. "What happened?"

"We don't know yet, but the important thing is that everyone's okay." Mama smiled through the tears still running down her cheeks.

I leaned my head back then, and looked at the ceiling. In my mind, I said to God, *Thank you! Thank you! Thank you!* And also, *Sorry! Sorry! Sorry!*

Chapter Six

Buzz and I were sharing corncakes in the kitchen on Thursday morning, June 6th, when the door to the basement squeaked open.

I turned around in my seat.

Pate poked his head out and looked around.

"He's already gone," Mama said, placing her skillet in the dishwasher.

"Huh?" Pate said.

Mama closed the dishwasher and turned to Pate. "Your father. He's already gone to work."

Pate came out from behind the door, shrugging his shoulders like, *Whatever.*

Mama handed him a plate. "And not coming out

of the basement except to eat, Pate, won't make us forget that you're down there."

Pate's cheeks turned pink. "Just tryin' to stay out of the way," he mumbled.

"You're not in the way," Mama said.

After Pate settled at the table and began eating, Mama dried her hands on her apron, picked up the phone, and began to dial.

"Hello, Trina," she said, and I knew then that Mama was talking to Mrs. Snopes, the choir director.

"This is Libby Morgan." Pause. "Yes, I know. We were so blessed. Actually, that's why I'm calling. I believe that your decision to hold auditions for choir saved my life, and the life of my daughter, and I want to thank you — " Long pause. "Oh? Well, I see." Pause. "Yes, of course, I'll be sure to thank her, too — she lives just next door, you know." Pause. "Yes, I will. Thank you again, Trina." Pause. "God bless you, too. Bye now."

Before Mama could even hang up the phone, I was banging my fist on the table. "I knew it! It was all Mrs. Peck's fault! She was the one that — "

"Fault?" Mama said, giving me a sharp look.

I closed my mouth.

Pate lowered his head so we couldn't see his face under the bill of his baseball cap, and he kept eating.

Mama put a hand on her hip and said, "Jamie Jo, whatever you may think, the truth is that those auditions saved our lives. *Mrs. Peck* saved our lives."

"I thought God saved our lives," I said.

"He did, but he wasn't working alone. Mrs. Peck helped him, and so did Mrs. Snopes."

I wasn't so sure about that.

"Jamie Jo, have you ever known me to be late for choir?" Mama said.

"No, ma'am," I said.

Mama nodded. "The only way I wouldn't show up for choir practice on time is if I wasn't *in* the choir."

I sat there and thought about that. I thought about it until Mama handed me the flyswatter and said, "Take Buzz outside now. He just ate."

"*Another* strawberry pie?" I said later that morning, when I brought Buzz back inside for about the twentieth time.

Mama smiled. "I know. We had more strawberries in the backyard this year than I knew what to do with. I'm glad this is the last of them."

I nodded and said, "They were good, Mama."

Not that I wanted any more of them. I was strawberried out, too. Over the last couple of weeks, Mama had served strawberries in one form or another at almost every meal.

"Let's hope that Mrs. Peck likes them," Mama said.

"The pie's for her?"

"Yes, Jamie Jo," Mama said impatiently. "See if you can get Buzz settled in his kennel, and then we'll take the pie next door."

"Do I *have* to go?" I said. I was glad that Mrs. Peck was okay and everything, but I still didn't like her.

Mama gave me a look that meant, *You're going.*

Mrs. Peck looked a little annoyed when she answered the door. "Yes?" she said, like she had never seen us before in her life. Or like she was about to say, *No, I don't wish to buy any pie today.*

"Jamie Jo and I just came over to give you this pie,

and to thank you for saving our lives," Mama said, getting right to it.

Mrs. Peck pushed her eyebrows together, and wrinkles appeared on her forehead. "I . . . I don't understand," she said.

"The auditions," Mama said. "The auditions saved our lives."

Mrs. Peck narrowed her eyes suspiciously and glared at Mama through her glasses. "Is this some sort of joke?"

Mama drew back, shocked. "No. No, not at all."

Mrs. Peck's face and eyes seemed to soften then. She took the pie and stepped back. "Forgive me. Please, come in."

Mama placed her hand on my back and ushered me inside.

"Please make yourselves comfortable," Mrs. Peck said. "I'm just going to put this in the refrigerator. Thank you."

Mama perched on the edge of a sofa covered in deep-pink roses, and I sat down beside her.

There were little round lace thingies all over the

place, on armrests and headrests and tables, under books and figurines and framed pictures. I looked up at Mama.

"Doilies," she whispered.

I nodded like I knew what that meant.

Mama and I sat there for a long time, waiting for Mrs. Peck to come back from the kitchen. But she didn't.

Mama nudged me. "Go check on her, Jamie Jo. Maybe she's making coffee or tea. Ask her if there's anything you can do to help."

I didn't want to, so I begged Mama with my eyes.

"Go on now," Mama whispered.

I crept across the living room and peeked into the kitchen. Mrs. Peck was sitting at the table, crying into her hands.

Quietly, I hurried back to Mama. "She's crying!"

"Crying as in . . . *crying?*" Mama whispered.

I nodded.

I followed Mama to the kitchen but stayed back in the doorway.

Mama pulled out the chair across from Mrs. Peck and sat down.

Mrs. Peck looked up then, and shook her head. "I'm sorry," she said.

"How can I help?" Mama asked.

Mrs. Peck wiped her eyes with a handkerchief that looked a lot like her doilies. "You can't," she said. "I've done it to myself. You understand?"

"I don't," Mama said gently, "but I'd like to."

Mrs. Peck tried to get a hold of herself. She sniffed, took a couple of deep breaths, and sat up straighter. "I've always been very critical, not just of other people, but of myself, too."

Mama nodded in her understanding way.

"It's isn't like I criticize just for the sake of it. I'm *trying* to be helpful, constructive."

"Well, of course you are," Mama said kindly.

Mrs. Peck seemed encouraged by this, and she continued, "I strive to be better . . . I strive for perfection, and I expect everyone around me to strive for perfection, too." Fresh tears began to fill her eyes, as she shook her head and added, "And to *keep* striving for it."

"That's not so bad," Mama said.

Mrs. Peck held up a finger and said, "It *is* bad, and I'll tell you why. Nobody ever *reaches* perfection — not at all things, all the time. There's always room for improvement somewhere."

"That's true," Mama said.

"So, I guess . . ." Mrs. Peck lowered her head and drew a ragged breath. The tears in her eyes dropped, first one, then the other, *plink, plink,* onto the kitchen table.

Mama reached across the table and placed her hand on top of Mrs. Peck's.

"So I guess . . . no one could ever really please me, because they never reached absolute perfection." Mrs. Peck looked up then, into Mama's face. She begged Mama to say something with her sad eyes, but Mama didn't.

Mrs. Peck lowered her head again, as she said softly, "And I guess eventually everyone got tired of trying, tired of being criticized. And they left me."

I could tell that Mama didn't know what to say to that. I didn't know either.

Mrs. Peck started to cry again. "I don't have any friends. My daughter, Annie, left home as soon as she could, and went as far away as she could. She went all the way to California for college, and she hasn't been home in years. Sometimes I think my husband died just to get away from me!"

"I'm sure that isn't so," Mama said.

"It is," Mrs. Peck wailed. "Believe me, I've had a lot of time to think about it, *years* to think about it. But did it change me? No. I still wanted perfection. So, I went after it at church, with the choir."

"I see," Mama said.

"Your singing was just so terrible, and so loud. I'm sorry, but it's true. We never could have gotten anywhere near perfection with *you* in the choir, so I came up with the idea of auditions." Mrs. Peck sobbed. "And then, I just wore Trina down over time."

Mama threw back her head and laughed.

Mrs. Peck looked confused at first but then she started laughing, too.

When the laughter died down, Mrs. Peck's face turned sad again. She sighed. "And now, here you are with a pie, thanking me for being the critical, judgmental, terrible person that I am. It's almost too much for me to take."

"I'm sorry," Mama said right away. "I didn't mean to hurt you."

Mrs. Peck shook her head. "No, I hurt *you*, and everyone else around me. And now I've lost the only thing I had left: my church. Now I'm truly and completely alone." She started to sob again.

Mrs. Peck cried so hard that her shoulders jerked up and down, and it kind of scared me.

It must've scared Mama, too, because she said, "Let me call someone for you. Why don't we call your daughter?"

"No," Mrs. Peck wailed. "Annie won't come. We had an argument yesterday morning."

"I'm sure it was nothing," Mama said.

"No . . . it was definitely *something*. Annie told me to mind my own business and I hung up on her. I didn't know what else to do! I certainly didn't raise her to be disrespectful like that — I never would've spoken to *my* mother like that!"

A little snot bubble formed around Mrs. Peck's left nostril, and I had to look away to keep from giggling. I busied myself with counting the little squares on the linoleum until I got hold of myself. When I looked up, thank goodness, the snot bubble was gone.

"How about Trina?" Mama suggested. "I'm sure she'd be glad to come over and keep you company for a while."

Mrs. Peck shook her head, and kept right on crying. "She only put up with me because of church! One has to put up with everybody at church!"

"Well, you shouldn't be alone," Mama said.

Mrs. Peck didn't argue, but she didn't tell Mama who she might call, either.

Finally, Mama said, "Why don't you come over for dinner at our house tonight?"

Mrs. Peck quieted, and blinked the tears from her eyes. "Thank you," she said.

Mama smiled, and pushed back from the table. "Six o'clock?"

Mrs. Peck nodded. Then she wiped her eyes and nose with her doily-handkerchief, picked her glasses up off the table, and put them back on.

"We'll be looking forward to seeing you," Mama said, coming to stand beside me.

"Say, would you like a piece of that strawberry pie, Jessie Jo?" Mrs. Peck said.

"No, thank you," I said.

"You really should eat," Mrs. Peck said to me, and then to Mama, "She *really* should."

I could kind of see Annie's point. *Mind your own business!* I thought to myself. To tell the truth, I'd had nicer feelings toward her when she was crying.

It was 6:26 when Daddy arrived home from work that night. He looked a little surprised when he walked into the kitchen and found us all eating dinner without him. He looked *really* surprised to see Mrs. Peck.

"Mrs. Peck, you remember my husband, James," Mama said, getting up.

"Please, call me Bea," Mrs. Peck said.

"Hello, Bea," Daddy said, taking his seat at the table.

"Your name is *Bee?*" I blurted out. *How awful!*

"Jamie Jo!" Mama scolded.

"Sorry," I said.

"My name is Beatrice," Mrs. Peck said, "but my friends call me Bea."

"Oh," I said. "Well, do you mind if I just call you Mrs. Peck?" At least it was her name, unlike Jessie Jo, which was *not* mine.

"Not at all, Jessie Jo," Mrs. Peck said.

Pate smirked at me.

Mama placed Daddy's plate on the table in front of him and sat back down.

"I'm sorry I'm late," Daddy said. "I stopped by the church on my way home."

"And?" Mama said.

Everyone stared at Daddy.

He shook his head. "There's nothing left. The explosion was so powerful, it knocked out the windows in many of the surrounding houses."

Everyone looked sad except for Pate, who could never be sad with a plate of food in front of him.

"And I spoke with the fire chief," Daddy said. "He

believes there was a damaged pipe that was leaking gas, and that when the gas reached the pilot light on the water heater, it caused the explosion."

Mrs. Peck set her fork down. "You know, I did the math," she said. "I figured that every member of the choir, except for you, Libby, was late for choir practice about once a month. That's one in four times."

"That sounds about right," Mama said.

Mrs. Peck nodded. "So the chances of everyone being late on the same night were around one in a million. It really was a miracle!"

The table was quiet while everyone thought about that.

Then Mama said brightly, "Jamie Jo loves math."

"That's wonderful," said Mrs. Peck, probably because she was a retired math teacher. "My daughter, Annie, loved math, too. And she's a doctor now!"

Throughout the remainder of dinner, Mama asked questions about Annie. I was kind of embarrassed. "Is Annie married?" "Where does she work?" "What city is that in?" "Does Annie live there or in the suburbs?" She was being downright nosy!

But I forgave Mama for her nosiness at exactly 9:14 that night, when I heard her on the phone in the kitchen.

"I'm sure," Mama said. "She'll be so glad to see you, Annie. I promise. People can change. Your mother wants to change. I know she's *trying*. She just needs a little help, a second chance. She needs a reason to try harder."

Chapter Seven

At 9:51 on Friday morning, June 7th, Buzz had his first accident in the house. Maybe "accident" isn't the right word because what Buzz did seemed pretty deliberate. He walked over to the floor-length velvet drapes in the living room, lifted his leg, and began peeing on them.

I saw him a second or two before Mama did.

"Buzz!" I shouted.

"Jamie Jo!" Mama shouted.

How was this my fault? *I* wasn't the one peeing on the drapes.

"Out! Out! Both of you!" Mama said. "Out! Now!"

I really didn't see how taking Buzz outside would help anything. After all, Buzz didn't have to go to the bathroom *now*. But since I could see that Mama was upset, I decided that outside with the bees was probably a safer place for us. So I scooped Buzz up, grabbed the flyswatter, and skedaddled out the door.

I sat down on the front steps, keeping an eye out for bees, while Buzz chased a butterfly in the grass. (See? I told you he didn't have to go.)

At 10:07, Rafi crossed the street. She stopped to pet Buzz. "I think he's grown already," she said, coming up the front walk.

"Grown fatter, that's what Daddy says," I said.

Rafi raised a hand to shield her eyes from the sun as she paused to look back at Buzz. "Yeah, could be."

I nodded, thinking back to how the book said that you should never feed your dog people-food or table scraps.

Rafi came to a stop in front of me. "My mom said I could invite you over to hang out and play, and eat lunch. We're having pizza."

"Thanks. Um, I just have to ask Mama," I said, without getting up.

"Okay, I'll wait right here," Rafi said.

"Well, I think maybe we'd both better wait," I said.

"How come?"

"She's kind of mad right now. Buzz just peed on the drapes."

"Oh," Rafi said, and she plopped down beside me on the step. "How long do you think we'll have to wait?"

"I don't know," I said. "I've never had a dog before. How long do *you* think we'll have to wait?"

"Depends," Rafi said.

"On what?" I asked.

"How much does she like the drapes?"

I swallowed hard. "She loves them. She *made* them."

Rafi sucked in air through her teeth. It wasn't very encouraging.

We both sat there, waiting, until I said, "I know! Maybe you could come inside with me, while I talk to Mama. She'd never be rude or mad or anything like that in front of a guest."

"Brilliant plan," Rafi said.

We found Mama standing on a chair in the living

room taking down the drapes. She didn't look happy. That is, she didn't look happy until she saw Rafi. Then she smiled sweetly down at us, and we knew that we had her. Mama even agreed to watch Buzz while I went to Rafi's!

"Cool!" I said, as soon as I stepped inside Rafi's bedroom, and it really was.

The walls were a bright spring-green, a color Mama calls new-growth-green, and loves to see in her garden. The bedspread was a deep purple, the color of my used-to-be favorite sundress.

Rafi threw herself onto the bed. I sat down next to Crooner, who was napping on a light purple rug beside Rafi's bed.

"Purple's my favorite color," I said.

"Mine too," Rafi said.

There was an awkward silence as Rafi stared at me. I busied myself with petting Crooner, and decided that Rafi was probably looking at my bones. *If only I hadn't worn shorts*, I thought. I tried to think of something unrelated to bones to say. *Bones, bones, bones* was all I could think of.

"Can I ask you something?" Rafi said, rolling onto her stomach.

"Go ahead," I said, hoping that she wasn't about to ask me something like, *Do you eat?* But it was far worse than that.

"How come you always carry a flyswatter around with you?"

I shrugged my shoulders and tried to make myself sound as casual as possible, like Pate. "I don't really like bugs."

"Me neither," Rafi said.

Since that had gone so well, I added, "And I hate bees."

"Me, too," Rafi said easily.

I took a deep breath then, and admitted, "And I'm a little scared of them. Bees."

Rafi nodded. "I'm a little scared of bees, too. But I'm really scared of burglars."

"Burglars?" I said.

"Yeah, you know, bad guys in ski masks that break into your house at night to steal stuff."

I watched Rafi carefully, trying to decide whether

or not she was teasing me. But she looked sincere. So I sat there thinking about burglars and ski masks.

Finally, I said, "Well, if I had to wear a ski mask inside a house, I'd pick a house with air conditioning."

Rafi propped her chin on her hands, and thought about that. "Nah," she decided out loud, "burglars don't care about stuff like air-conditioning. They only care about stuff like jewelry and good silver."

I decided the Yells must've had a lot of jewelry and "good" silver, whatever that was.

Then Rafi added, "And burglars are so quiet, you don't even know they're in your house until you bump into them. That's why I stay in my bed all night, no matter what. I don't want to bump into any burglars."

"But what if you *really* have to go to the bathroom?"

Rafi shook her head. "I just don't do it. I go right before bed, and that's it. I don't get up again for anything. Because you just never know."

"That *is* scary," I said.

"Seriously."

"Do your parents know about burglars?" I asked. After all, parents are supposed to protect you — even when it means carrying a lime-green flyswatter everywhere!

Rafi rolled her eyes. "They say I have an 'overactive imagination.'"

I thought about burglars some more, and then said, "Maybe I could ask Mama if you could come and stay at our house. I don't think we have a lot of jewelry or good silver."

"Thanks, but it wouldn't do any good. Burglars can break in anywhere anytime, and they don't know what you've got until they're inside your house."

Huh? I stopped petting Crooner then, and started to worry a little about burglars.

A few minutes passed, and then Rafi said, "So, what do you do for fun around here?"

"Um . . . well, we *used* to go to church," I said.

"Used to?"

"Yeah," I said, and then I told her about the explosion at church. I told her how everyone in the choir had been late, except for Mama who'd been fired from the choir the week before, and definitely would've been there on time otherwise.

"How come everybody else was late?" Rafi asked. "Were they all together somewhere?"

"No," I said. "One lady was taking a nap and her alarm clock never went off. Two people had car trouble, and two more people were supposed to ride to church with them. One man decided to finish watching a TV show that wasn't over until 6:30. Another man was writing an email and forgot about the time. Mrs. Snopes, the choir director, decided to iron her daughter's dress just as they were walking out the door. I can't remember what else, but it was all just regular stuff like that."

"Wow," Rafi said, her eyes wide.

"Yeah," I said.

"Well, maybe when you go back to church, I could come with you," Rafi said.

"Sure," I said.

"Would I have to wear a dress?" Rafi said, crinkling her nose. "I don't like dresses. I don't even have one."

I shrugged. "You can wear pants if you want to, or you can borrow a dress from me."

"Hey, did you ever hear them talk about Saint Ends at your church?" Rafi asked.

I shook my head. "No. I know Saint Peter, but I've never heard of any Saint Ends. Who is he?"

"I don't know. That's why I asked *you*."

"Well, where did you hear about Saint Ends?" I said.

Rafi got up, and Crooner lifted her head, like, *Are we leaving?*

The jewelry box on Rafi's dresser played music when she opened it, and a ballerina pirouetted in front of a little round mirror inside the box. Rafi closed it, and the ballerina disappeared as the music stopped.

"I've always wanted one of those," I said.

Rafi handed me a silver chain from her jewelry box, and sat down beside me on the rug. Crooner laid her head back down.

"See?" Rafi said, "It says 'Saint Ends.'"

I looked at the upside-down tear-shaped charm

on the necklace. Stacked on top of each other were the words ST ENDS.

That's when I knew Rafi and I were going to be best friends. I just *knew.* "Did you get this out of the quarter machine at Wheeler's Drugstore?" I asked.

"Yeah."

I nodded and handed the necklace back to her. "It's supposed to be part of a set. The other half of the charm says BE FRI, and when you put them together, they form a heart that says, BEST FRIENDS."

"Ooooohhh," Rafi said.

For a minute, I thought she might put the necklace on. She looked like she wanted to, but then Rafi placed the necklace carefully on her nightstand.

Why, oh why, had I wasted my quarters on giant gumballs the one and only time that Mama let me have money for the junk machines? After all, I didn't need four gumballs. No one needs *four;* you can barely chew *one!* No, what I needed was a BE FRI necklace!

"Pizza!" Mrs. Yell hollered from downstairs.

My heart leapt when I saw the box on the kitchen table. *Hunt Brothers Pizza.*

"Oh my gosh!" I said to Rafi. "This is the best pizza in the South, maybe the best in the world!"

"Seriously," Rafi said, smiling a crooked half-smile.

"Seriously?" I said.

Rafi nodded. "Seriously. It means, like, *I know.*"

Over lunch, I said, "So, like, what do you like to do?"

Rafi thought about it while she chewed. "I like roller-skating, basketball, four-square, swimming. Hey, does your neighbor let you swim in her pool?"

I shook my head.

Rafi looked disappointed.

To be honest, I was disappointed, too, because so far, I was pretty sure that every activity Rafi had named was an *outside* activity. Outside, as in where bees live.

"Um, what do you do when it rains?" I asked, reaching for another slice of pizza.

"I like movies and music . . . Oh! And I like tape."

"Tape?"

"Yeah, you know, like Scotch tape?" Rafi said.

Now that I was thinking about it, tape was pretty fun. I nodded my head. "Tape's good."

"Seriously."

As soon as I got home I asked Mama, "Do we have any good silver?"

"Of course," Mama said, as she ran her feather duster over the table in the front hall. "Most of it came from your great-grandmother, Lucille. When your father and I . . ."

I didn't hear anything else Mama said. I was too busy thinking about burglars.

I met Daddy at the front door when he arrived home from work at 5:22.

"Have you put a lot of burglars in jail?" I asked, tapping my toe impatiently. I'd been waiting for Daddy all afternoon.

He slowed and looked confused. "Uh . . . some. Why do you ask?"

My toe stopped tapping. His question slowed me down, too. I wasn't sure how to answer it. I didn't feel right telling Daddy about Rafi's fear. I sure didn't want her to go around telling people about *my* fear!

Daddy set his briefcase down.

"Burglars are scary," was all I said.

Daddy thought about it and then said, "Yes, they can be. But do you know what scares burglars?"

"What?"

"Dogs," Daddy said simply. "Burglars don't bother houses that have dogs."

Of course! I nodded and promised myself I'd remember to tell Rafi.

After dinner, I was standing in the front yard waiting for Buzz to do his business when a yellow taxi pulled up in front of Mrs. Peck's house at 7:17. A pretty woman with black hair got out of the cab. She had a suitcase with her and as soon as I saw it, I knew she had to be Annie, Mrs. Peck's daughter.

It had been such a good day (except for the incident with the drapes) and I was so happy that I felt downright friendly! So I waved to Annie.

I watched Annie knock on Mrs. Peck's door. Can you imagine knocking on your own front door?

After a minute, Mrs. Peck opened the door wearing a pink bathrobe. For a split-second, I don't think Mrs. Peck recognized Annie, but when she did, she threw her arms around her and began to cry.

Who would've guessed that such a mean old woman would do so much crying? Not me, that's for sure.

Chapter Eight

At breakfast the following Sunday morning, June 9th, Mama set her coffee cup down and said to Pate, "I've decided where I want my flowers."

His mouth was full of sausage and gravy, so Pate nodded for Mama to continue.

"I think we should make another large flower bed along the back by the birdhouse."

Pate swallowed. "Yeah, I kinda figured we'd have to dig another bed when I came home and saw all the flowers and stuff sittin' at the end of the driveway yesterday."

On Saturday, the nursery had delivered enough plants, flowers, bushes, and flowering trees for us to start our own nursery.

"We're going to need mulch," Mama said, looking hopefully at Daddy.

When Daddy looked up from his plate and saw Mama staring at him like that, he said, "The truck's already parked."

Pate rolled his eyes.

"Have it delivered," Daddy said, stabbing his sausage with his fork.

"They don't deliver on Sundays," Pate said.

"Tomorrow then," Daddy said.

"Pate won't be here to help me tomorrow. He has to go back over to the Garrett place," Mama said. "Besides, I want to get it done today. There's a chance of rain tomorrow."

Daddy set his jaw and said again, "The truck's already *parked*."

I knew that was the end of it. Apparently, Mama and Pate knew it, too, because no one said anything else during breakfast.

When Mama came in from the backyard, I had just finished giving Buzz a bath in the kitchen sink. Okay, okay, so I hadn't bathed him *every* day like I'd promised, but Buzz really hadn't started to stink until yesterday.

Mama took off her big straw hat and hung it on the hook by the back door.

"It's 11:11!" I announced. 11:11 is my favorite time because it's the only time that consists of four numbers that are all the same. Think about it: Is there a 22:22 or a 33:33? Pretty cool, huh?

Mama smiled and pulled off her gardening gloves. "We'll celebrate with sweet tea."

I got out the big pot while Mama washed her hands. I was known for being quite helpful when it came to sweet tea (and ice cream sundaes).

At 11:28 Mama was pouring our sweet tea into a pitcher filled with ice.

She gave me the first glass, and made two more glasses, which she carried out the back door.

The first thing I heard was the sound of glass breaking. The second thing I heard was Mama screaming.

I raced out onto the back porch, and something crunched under my feet. I looked down at the spilled tea and broken glass. When I looked up, I saw them: Pate was lying on his back in the grass while Mama crouched over him screaming for help. She looked over and saw me. "Get your father!" she hollered.

I ran back inside screaming, "Daddy! Daddy! Daddy! Daddy!" all through the house. Then I was out the front door and running through the yard, to Mrs. Peck's house.

Annie answered the door.

"Come! Come right now!" I said before I took off running again.

She must have known I meant business, because when I got to Mama and Daddy and Pate in the back-yard, Annie was right behind me.

Annie dropped to her knees in the grass beside Pate. "Medical conditions, allergies?" she barked, swatting impatiently at a bee buzzing around her face.

I scurried behind Daddy, daring only to peek out through the little space left between his arm and his body. I knew Annie was asking for trouble, the way she was swatting at that bee. And I figured we all looked about the same to bees. I surely did not want to be mistaken for Annie by an angry bee!

"Not that we know of," Mama said, sitting back on her heels.

Daddy covered the mouthpiece of the phone he was holding to his ear. "I have the 911 operator on the line. She's sending an ambulance."

Annie ignored Daddy, took hold of Pate's wrist, and leaned over to listen near his face.

I doubted that she could hear anything over Buzz, who was barking and growling at the birdhouse.

Pate was perfectly still. *Too* still. His eyes were closed and his lips were a bluish color. It was the worst, scariest thing I'd ever seen.

I started to tremble and cry.

Daddy pulled what looked like a fat pen out of his pocket, and held it out to Annie. "Uh . . . do you think . . . ?"

Before he could even finish, Annie had grabbed the pen, yanked the top off, and jabbed it into Pate's thigh.

I mashed my face into Daddy's white shirt and cried even harder. I shouldn't have gotten Annie, I realized then. After all, Pate was already hurt, and now she'd gone and *stabbed* him with a huge pen!

"Tell the operator to cancel the ambulance," Annie said. "We're already here and we have a car."

Annie swept her fingers through Pate's mouth, and then put her mouth over Pate's and started breathing into him. When she stopped, she put her hands on his chest and pumped — hard. "Go get the float by our pool and bring it here," she said.

Daddy tossed the phone in the grass and took off across the yard, running faster than I'd ever seen him run.

Annie kept breathing and pumping on Pate. It didn't seem to me that she was helping very much. I mean, first she'd stabbed him, and now she was practically beating him up!

"Please, Lord!" Mama shouted at the blue sky.

Buzz kept right on barking at the birdhouse.

And then Pate coughed. I never thought I'd be so happy to hear a cough! When Daddy came back with the float, Mama said, "James, he coughed! He coughed!"

Annie said calmly, "Now, we're going to roll him onto the float and put him in the back of your truck, as fast as we can."

Mama and I took one end of the float, while Daddy and Annie took the other. We moved carefully and quickly.

Once Pate was lying flat on the float in the bed of Daddy's truck, Annie climbed in beside him. "Take it easy," she said in a soft, soothing voice. "Slow, deep breaths. That's it."

Daddy hopped into the driver's seat while Mama and I ran around the truck and jumped in on the other side. We barely had the door closed when the truck lurched forward.

I squeezed my eyes shut, and prayed all the way to the hospital.

Annie sat beside Mama, holding her hand, in the hospital waiting room. Daddy sat on Mama's other side, with me in his lap.

It seemed like we were there waiting for days.

There were two other families in the waiting

room. I noticed that we all had the same frightened looks on our faces.

There was a television, which was on, but nobody was watching it. Instead, we all watched the door.

Suddenly, I remembered Buzz. "Oh my gosh! We left Buzz out in the backyard! I have to call Rafi!" I said, hopping down off Daddy's lap.

Daddy reached into his pocket, pulled out a fistful of change, and shoved all of it at me.

"I'll go with her," Annie said.

After I explained the situation to Rafi, she said, "Do you want me to ask my mom to drive me to the hospital?"

"*What?* No, just get Buzz," I said, wondering why on earth she would ask me such a thing. Why would Rafi want to come to the hospital? After all, hospitals aren't fun. And anyway, I didn't have time for fun right now.

I was still wondering about it when we returned to the waiting room. I climbed back onto Daddy's lap.

A few minutes later, Daddy whispered to Mama, "One of us should call Vicky. Whatever's going on between them, she's still Pate's wife . . . in sickness and in health."

"I'll do it," Mama said, getting up from her seat.

When Mama returned to the waiting room, the first thing she said was, "Any news?"

Everybody shook their heads.

Mama sat back down and leaned over, close to Daddy. In a voice barely above a whisper, she said, "For future reference, Vicky *isn't* Pate's wife anymore. In fact, she hasn't seen him in more than two months."

"Well, is she coming, or isn't she?" Daddy said, like somehow that was what really mattered.

Mama shook her head. "She isn't."

Daddy grunted.

After a while, Daddy said to no one in particular, "Pate deserves better."

I didn't know whether he was talking about the sickness or Vicky, but either way I decided he was right. Pate didn't deserve to be sick any more than he deserved a wife who didn't like him. After all, if she'd liked him even a teensy little bit, she would've come to the hospital, right?

Then all at once, I understood why Rafi had offered to come. She liked me! We really were best friends, or on our way to becoming best friends, at least. For a split second I felt happy. But then I remembered poor Pate and felt ashamed. How could I be happy *here, now?* What in the world was wrong with me?

Finally, a doctor appeared, and everyone in the waiting room looked up hopefully. "Morgan family?" the doctor said.

Daddy moved me into the empty chair on his other side, and stood up.

The doctor came over to us. "Bees," he said simply. "Your boy's allergic to bee stings. But he's going to be just fine, thanks to Dr. Peck here."

Daddy shook the doctor's hand.

I offered Annie a forgiving smile.

"Can we see him?" Mama said, clasping her hands together in front of her.

We followed the doctor down the hall.

"Thank The Lord we weren't at church," Mama said.

"Thank The Lord Annie was next door," I said.

"Thank The Lord the truck was parked in the driveway," Daddy said.

We all laughed nervously, even Annie.

When the doctor stopped walking and pointed to a door on our right, Annie said, "I think I'll go get some coffee. Does anyone else want some?"

No one did.

Pate was sitting up and talking to a nurse when we entered his room. "Hey," he said, smiling when he saw all of us.

Mama rushed to hug Pate's neck.

Daddy shook Pate's hand.

I bounced on the end of his bed, just a little, and waited.

Pate winked at me.

I smiled at him, and squeezed one of his feet through the scratchy white sheet that I knew would've given *me* a rash all over my body.

When everyone was quiet and settled, I said, "See? I told y'all that bees were bad."

Mama and Daddy exchanged worried looks.

"You were right, Mama. There's purpose in all things," I said proudly. "It all makes sense now, doesn't it?"

I figured that Mama had probably saved my life *hundreds* of times with her flyswatter.

"Yeah," Pate said. "There're a bunch of bees living in the birdhouse. When I was working out back, I accidentally bumped it, and that's when they all came out and started stinging me."

"They'll be gone before you get home," Daddy assured him.

"Well, don't kill 'em, Dad," Pate said. "Call a beekeeper. Bees *aren't* bad."

Daddy opened his mouth. He looked ready to argue the virtues of bees, but there was a knock on the door, and he closed it again.

"Come in," Mama called.

Annie pushed the door open and poked her head in. "Hi," she said.

Mama got up and ushered Annie to Pate's bedside. "I don't believe you've been properly introduced.

This is Annie Peck, Mrs. Peck's daughter. She saved your life, Pate."

"Uh, thank you," Pate said nervously as he reached up and started combing his hair with his fingers.

"You're welcome," Annie said. "So. If it's all right with you all, I met a doctor in the cafeteria who offered to give me a ride."

"No!" Pate said, loudly. "Uh . . . I mean . . . it's just that . . . well, I'm sure Dad can give you a ride."

We all stared at Pate.

Annie smiled at him. "I promise you're in good hands here."

"I'll walk you out," Mama said, shaking her head at Pate, just barely. It was the old *Stop-it* or *Drop-it* look.

In this case, I was guessing Mama meant *Stop it!*

I wanted Pate to stop it, too. He was acting so weird!

When Mama came back from walking Annie out, she had papers with her.

"Do I get to go home now?" Pate said hopefully.

"Can we stop by the drugstore on the way home?" I asked, because I still had two quarters mixed in with all the change Daddy had given me, and I really needed that *BE FRI* necklace.

Mama ignored me. "No, Pate, you can't go yet. They're going to keep you for observation." Then she held up the papers in her hand. "These are for the allergist that you and Jamie Jo will be seeing in a few days."

Pate sighed like it was no use, and dropped his head back onto his pillow.

I pretended to pout a little, because nobody had answered me.

Then Daddy said quietly, "We called Vicky, son."

Pate bit his lip, and turned away.

"Where were you staying before you came home?" Mama said.

Pate shrugged. "Oh, you know. I crashed with friends, and hung out in the back room at the Yamaha music store, here and there . . . you know."

Mama gave Daddy a look that meant: *this is your fault.*

Chapter Nine

Mama dropped Daddy off at work on Wednesday, June 12th, so that she could drive Pate and me to our appointment with Dr. Goodman, the allergist.

Of course, it turned out that Pate *was* allergic to bee stings, but not as highly allergic as we'd thought. Dr. Goodman said that Pate would be fine, as long as he wasn't attacked by an entire colony of bees and stung multiple times, like had happened on Sunday. But he also gave Pate a shot, which looked like the fat pen Annie had poked him with, to carry around, just in case a colony showed up.

Of course, I didn't need any doctor to tell me that one bee sting would kill me in seconds. I already knew it.

Except that I was wrong.

When I was called back to Dr. Goodman's office at 11:53, he said, "You're no more allergic to bee stings than the average person."

I shrugged. "So? A bee could still kill me. I am a highly sensitive person, just like Thomas in *My Girl.*"

Mama's head snapped up. "Thomas wasn't just *sensitive,* Jamie Jo. Thomas was *allergic.*"

I looked at her through squinty eyes. "Are you *sure?*"

"I'm positive."

"Well . . . then I am, too," I said to Mama. "I'm allergic, too, right?" I looked at Dr. Goodman, and waited for him to back me up here.

"Yes and no," the doctor said, with a grin that I found a little irritating, to be honest.

I gave him my squinty scowl. "How can it be yes *and* no?"

Mama crossed her arms and gave me her *Stop-it* or *Drop-it* headshake from the chair beside me.

I knew she meant *Stop it!* But I stared straight ahead and pretended not to see her.

The doctor chuckled. "I know what I'm doing," he said. "Hear me out, okay?"

I shrugged my shoulders and began inspecting my nails, like, *Well, okay, but only because I don't have anything better to do right this minute.*

"Almost everyone's allergic to bee stings, Jamie Jo," Doctor Goodman said. "That's why when a person gets stung, it involves some localized pain and swelling, but for most people that's all there is to it, a little pain and swelling."

"I am *not* most people," I informed him. "I am a highly sensitive person!"

"Jamie Jo Morgan!" Mama gasped.

Dr. Goodman chuckled again, and this time his belly shook. "Oh, I agree with you completely," he said. "But in terms of bee stings, you *are* most people — you might experience some pain and swelling, but nothing more than that."

"Are you saying that a bee sting wouldn't kill me?" I said, because that was just about the craziest thing I'd ever heard.

"It won't kill you," Dr. Goodman said certainly.

"How can you be sure?" I said. "I don't see any bees in here."

"The bees themselves aren't here, but their venom *is* here, and you've been stung several times today. You just didn't know it."

"You stung me?" I shrieked. "You could've killed me!"

Dr. Goodman laughed and said, "Extremely unlikely." Then he stood and said to Mama, "Tell Mr. Morgan I said hello."

I was mad at Dr. Goodman all the way home.

Mama was mad, too, only she was mad at me. Me!

"But he *stung* me!" I kept saying. "That isn't right!"

Pate laughed until tears ran from his eyes.

I decided that I was mad at Pate, too.

When we pulled into the driveway, Mama said, "Pate, would you take Buzz outside?"

"Sure."

After he closed the car door, Mama turned to me. "Why are you so mad, Jamie Jo?"

"Because he *stung* me!" I said again.

Mama took a deep breath, like she was trying to

hold something in. Then she said, "You may think that's why you're mad, but that isn't why. You didn't even know you'd been stung. You weren't hurt and you weren't in any danger of being hurt or killed."

"But — "

Mama held up a hand to stop me. "Not another word," she said, "not until you can tell me the real reason that you're so angry."

"I *am* — "

"Not. Another. Word."

I stayed in my room with the door shut all afternoon.

When I didn't come down for dinner, Mama came up to check on me.

I had planned to ignore her and stay mad but I couldn't on account of the fact that Mama happened to be holding a huge ice cream sundae.

I didn't mean to smile, but I accidentally did.

Mama smiled back, handed me the sundae, and sat down on the bed beside me.

"So?" she said.

"So how come Daddy has a fat pen like Pate's?"

Mama's forehead scrunched for a few seconds, but then her face relaxed again. "Oh, you mean the Epi-Pen. Your father's allergic to shellfish."

"What's shellfish?"

"Shrimp, oysters, crawfish. Any fish that comes in a shell."

"Oh," I said.

"So?" Mama tried again.

"So, um, what ever happened to the bees in the birdhouse?" I asked. "Did they die?"

"Only a few, only the ones Buzz ate. But a beekeeper came and collected the rest."

"Was he wearing a spacesuit when he came?"

"I wasn't here when *she* came. I was at the hospital with you and Pate," Mama said, "but I'm sure she wore a beekeeper's suit, which does look at little like a spacesuit."

"Cool," I said.

"So," Mama said again, only this time it wasn't a question.

"Well okay then," I huffed. "I'm mad because I've

been telling people for a whole year that one bee sting would kill me, and . . ." I shrugged.

Mama nodded. "And now you're wrong."

"Exactly!"

"I'd rather be wrong than be afraid," Mama said.

I had to think about that one for a while, which wasn't a bad thing because it gave me time to eat my ice cream.

When I finished, I set the empty bowl on my nightstand and whined, "I really *hate* being wrong."

"Oh, Jamie Jo, there are so many worse things."

"Like what?" I said.

"Like being afraid, or like being alone. Think about Mrs. Peck."

I didn't see what Mrs. Peck had to do with anything. "What about her?" I said.

"Well, she criticized the people around her all the time, and you know what?"

"What?"

"She was probably *right*. She was right about my singing. But sometimes, Jamie Jo, being right just isn't the important thing."

Chapter Ten

On Sunday evening, June 23rd, we were eating one of Mama's best dinners — roast beef, potatoes, carrots, and baked apples — in honor of Annie's last night in town, when I noticed that Pate was acting weirder than usual.

He looked sort of slouchy, or *sad,* or something. And when I looked at his plate, I realized that he had barely touched his food!

At exactly 6:42, just as I decided that Pate was sick, Annie said, "I have a little announcement to make."

Everyone looked at Annie and she smiled.

"You should be on a toothpaste commercial," I told her.

"Thank you," she said to me. Then, to everyone

else, "As you all know, I'll be returning to California in the morning."

Everyone nodded, and I think we all looked pretty sorry about that.

"What you *don't* know is that I'm only going back in order to resign, work out my notice, and pack up my life. Then I'll be back — the doctor who drove me home from the hospital when Pate was stung offered me a job!"

Tears filled Mrs. Peck's eyes. "Back? Back *here?* To stay?"

Annie nodded. "If you'll have me, Mom. I'll need a place to stay for a little while."

"Does this mean we can swim in your pool?" I asked, because after all, Annie and I were friends now. And ever since I'd learned that bees couldn't kill me, I'd had my eye on that pool.

But Annie only glanced at me.

Mrs. Peck set her fork down and pulled one of her doily-handkerchiefs out of her sleeve as the tears spilled from her eyes.

Mama smiled warmly at Mrs. Peck. Daddy

nodded his head at Annie in approval. Pate looked like he'd been cured. He perked right up, like one of Mama's peace lilies that had only needed a little water.

"I'm staying, too," Pate said, wearing a goofy grin.

Mama looked a little worried then. Daddy sighed and his shoulders slumped.

"Just until I finish college," Pate explained.

Mama smiled hopefully at Daddy. Daddy raised one eyebrow at Pate.

"I'm majoring in horticulture this time," Pate added. Then he turned and said to Annie, "One day I'll own my own nursery and landscaping company."

"What's horticulture?" I asked.

"It's the science of raising and caring for garden plants," Mrs. Peck said in her teacher's voice.

"You're smart to stay at home, Pate," Annie said. "Good meals, clean laundry, no distractions."

Pate speared a hunk of roast beef with his fork and chewed thoughtfully. "Yeah, clean laundry's a big one. You know, I once had a roommate who got a note from the lady he paid to do his laundry. The note said,

'Please stop blowing your nose in your socks or take your laundry elsewhere.'"

Mama gasped, and gave Pate the *Stop-It* look.

In case that wasn't enough, I clutched the BE FRI necklace at my neck (which I'd gotten on the way home from the hospital, when we stopped to fill Pate's prescriptions). "That's gross, Pate. We're trying to eat here!"

Daddy pinched the bridge of his nose, like he was getting a headache.

But before anyone could say anything more, Annie's laughter had filled the room like music.

It must've been catchy, because pretty soon we were all laughing and smiling.

Apparently, Pate found this encouraging, because he continued to tell weird and funny stories, one right after another, for the rest of dinner.

When I wasn't laughing, I couldn't help wondering who in the world this guy was. He looked like my brother, he sounded like my brother, but he was definitely a *different* Pate.

When we finally started clearing the table, Annie

put a hand on her belly. "I've laughed so hard and so much, my stomach hurts."

Pate looked awfully pleased with himself.

At 10:23 that night, Pate slipped into my bedroom and closed the door behind him. He whispered into the darkness, "Can you hear them?"

I knew that he was talking about Mama and Daddy in the next room. I turned over in my bed. "Sometimes . . . sort of. Well, not really."

I heard my closet door open, and I knew what Pate was doing. My bedroom was connected to Mama and Daddy's bedroom by a deep closet with doors on both sides that we shared.

I heard hangers scraping against the wooden bar and shoes being kicked out of the way.

"Shhhh!" I hissed. "They'll hear you!"

"Come on," Pate whispered, climbing into the closet. "Lemme show you how it's done." (My room had been Pate's before I was born.)

Now, I have to admit that I knew it wasn't right to sit in the closet and eavesdrop on Mama and Daddy. But after all, Mama *had* said, "Sometimes being right just isn't the important thing," so I crawled into the closet with Pate and sat down.

"So what if he likes her? Don't you want him to be happy?" we heard Mama say.

OOOOooooh, I thought. *Pate likes Annie! He like-likes her. He wants her to be his girlfriend.*

"We're happy, and we only got married once," Daddy said.

"We were lucky," Mama said.

"No, I *knew,*" Daddy said.

"Well, I didn't," Mama said. "I could've easily made the same mistakes that Pate's made. Anybody could have and lots of people *do.*"

"'Lots of people' aren't my son," Daddy said. "What will other people think?"

"Since when do we live our lives and make decisions based on what 'other people' might think?" Mama said.

"I don't know, Libby," Daddy said.

"Just because Pate's made some mistakes, he doesn't deserve any more chances at happiness? He has to spend the rest of his life alone now, is that it?

He's finished at the age of twenty-two, because you're worried about what 'other people' think?"

"I don't know," Daddy said again.

"Well, *I* know," Mama said.

"What?" Daddy said. "What do you know, really know, for sure?"

"I know that your son would rather sleep in the back of a store front or on a friend's sofa than come home and admit to you that he made a mistake, and that he needs your help. What do you think 'other people' think about that?"

There was some huffing and puffing, and other angry sounds on the other side of the door, but nobody said anything else. A minute later, the crack of light under the closet door turned black.

I couldn't see Pate's face when we climbed out of the closet, but I could make out his form, like a shadow, in my room. And I could tell by the way he held himself that he was sad, maybe a little embarrassed, probably both.

"Hey, want to go to the basement and have a jam session?" I said.

"Nah," Pate said.

"How about an ice cream sundae?" I tried. After all, ice cream sundaes almost always made me feel better.

"Maybe later."

I climbed back into bed as Pate tiptoed to my door.

"Pate?" I whispered.

"Yeah?"

"Mama'll win him over in the end," I said. "She always does."

"I know," Pate said, "but I don't want Mama to have to win him over for me, you know?"

"What do you want then?"

The outline of Pate's shoulders moved up and down. "I don't know. I guess I want to win him over myself."

"Seriously," I said.

"Seriously?"

"It means, like, *I know*," I informed him.

"I know what it means, Squirt," Pate said, and I could hear the smile in his voice.

Chapter Eleven

Rafi and I spent nearly every waking minute together during the month of July. And together, we made sure that Buzz didn't have a single accident in the house! But we didn't accomplish much else. No one did. The month of July was so hot and humid that everyone tried not to move around too much, tried not to break a sweat. The sad truth is that when you don't have air-conditioning, you just can't get cooled off once you get too hot. I highly, *highly* recommend air-conditioning. Luckily, the diner is air-conditioned, so we ate dinner there, when Mama said it was too hot to turn the oven on — the oven makes our kitchen even hotter.

Anyway, on Friday morning, August 9th, Mrs. Yell, Mama, Rafi, and I all went to school together to register and meet the teachers. Rafi didn't seem to care that much about meeting her new teacher, but she was *desperate* to know if we'd be in the same class. I hoped we were, but I also hoped my teacher was nice, because a cranky teacher can just about ruin your whole year!

Rafi and I both wore our brand new, deep-purple Converse All-Stars (which we'd decided on the phone last night) and our BEST FRIENDS necklaces.

When we walked into the school, I made a face at Rafi. "Did your old school smell like this?" I asked her.

She took a deep breath through her nose. "Yeah."

I shook my head in disgust. "Why do schools have to smell so bad?" I wondered aloud.

"Seriously," Rafi said.

The good news was that Rafi and I would be in the same class this year. The bad news was that we would both have to suffer a whole year with Mrs. Shropshire as our teacher.

I knew I wasn't going to like Mrs. Shropshire the second I saw her shoes, which were black leather lace-ups with thick, rubber soles, like the ones old Miss Lurleen wears when she's working at the diner.

Shoes say a lot about a person, I tell you. For example, last year, I'd known I was going to love Miss Tucker, because when I'd gone to meet her, we were both wearing the exact same sandals! And I was right. Miss Tucker was the sweetest, prettiest teacher I ever had. She was the one that let me stay beside her on the teachers' bench during recess. But Mrs. Shropshire . . . well, I already knew she wasn't going to put up with that. I could tell. If her shoes weren't enough, when Rafi stuck a pencil in the fancy, electric pencil sharpener in Mrs. Shropshire's classroom (just to try it out) Mrs. Shropshire looked like her head might explode. "Stop that this instant!" she boomed. (See? I told you.)

"Mrs. Shropshire seems like a good teacher," Mama said, once we were all back outside. "Don't you think, Jamie Jo?"

I shook my head. "Did you see her *shoes?*"

Rafi giggled.

"Yes," Mama said, "and I think they're no-

nonsense. I like that. I think Mrs. Shropshire is a very no-nonsense kind of teacher."

"That's the problem!" I said.

Mama and Mrs. Yell exchanged a look.

That night, in honor of their anniversary, Mama made Daddy's favorite dinner: fried chicken with all the fixings.

"Mmmmm," Daddy said, biting into a chicken leg. His eyes were closed.

Mama smiled.

"I think this is the best fried chicken you've ever made, Libby."

"Thank you," Mama said.

"So, Pate, what are your plans this evening?" Daddy asked.

Pate looked up from his food like he was surprised to see the rest of us sitting at the table with him. (He loves fried chicken, too.) "Uh, well . . . I promised Annie I'd call at 8:00. Other than that, I'm just gonna study."

"Study?" Daddy said, doubtfully. "On a Friday night?"

"Yes, sir," Pate said.

Daddy broke into a wide smile that showed his teeth. (Daddy doesn't usually show his teeth when he smiles.) This meant that he was downright thrilled.

Buzz grew impatient and scratched at one of my legs under the table. But I ignored him. I like fried chicken, too.

When dinner was over, Daddy stood, thanked Mama, and looked at his watch. Then he disappeared down the hallway. A minute later, he called out, "Libby, if you can be ready in five minutes, we can just make a movie!"

Mama froze, holding a dinner plate, and her eyes widened.

My eyes widened, too. I was thinking, *But the truck's already parked!* Only I forgot all about that when Mama started moving again.

She tore her apron off and spread it out on the counter. Then, she stacked all the dirty dishes and silverware on top of her apron, folded the apron around everything, shoved the whole big, bundle *into the oven,* and shut the door!

My mouth dropped open.

Mama smiled a little smile at me and said, "Shhhhhh. It's our secret. Nobody'll ever know."

I nodded slowly.

"Well . . ." Mama said, looking at me, "they might suspect *something* if you don't close your mouth."

I closed it.

Mama fluffed her hair with her hands. "Lipstick! Lipstick! I need lipstick!"

On her way out the front door, Mama paused and whispered to Pate and me, "Whatever you do, *don't* turn on the oven."

I nodded.

Pate shrugged his shoulders, like, *Yeah, okay, whatever.* He didn't care. He didn't have any plans to turn the oven on. (Pate doesn't cook. He only eats.)

When Pate hung the phone up at 8:41, I cornered him in the kitchen. "Are you going to marry Annie?" I asked.

"What?" Pate said, shaking his head like that was just about the craziest thing he'd ever heard. "I don't know. We're only *dating*, Jamie Jo."

I put my hands on my hips. "Yeah, but haven't you married every girl you've dated?"

Pate started to shake his head again, but something slowed him down this time. He seemed to be thinking. Finally, he grinned and said, "Well . . . ya got me there, Squirt."

I knew it!

Chapter Twelve

Sunday, September 1st, was a day of many firsts. Since Rafi had spent the night for the first time the night before, she was there for several of them.

Our church was still in the process of being rebuilt, but the sanctuary had been completed, so we were having the first Sunday morning service at church since the explosion. I was glad because for the past few Sunday mornings, we'd had the service in the Ritchie family's living room, and their itchy blue carpet gave me a rash.

It wasn't even 9:30 yet when Mama began bustling around the house. She was even worse than usual! But when I heard the thunder rumbling in the distance, I understood. Mama wanted to get to church before it started raining, because of course, we were walking.

"Jamie Jo Morgan! Rafael Yell! I *will* leave here, with or without you at 10:00 sharp!" Mama hollered as she hurried up the stairs.

Rafi's eyes bulged and her mouth dropped open.

"Um, apparently you're not a guest anymore," I said. "This is normal behavior in my family."

Rafi tried on two more of my dresses before settling on my used-to-be favorite purple sundress, which she'd found at the very back of my closet.

"Oh, you don't want to wear that one," I told her.

"Why not?"

"It's a summer dress."

"Yeah, and it's still summer. The first day of fall isn't until the autumnal equinox, on September 22," Rafi said proudly, because we had just learned about the autumnal equinox in school.

I was thinking, trying to come up with another argument.

"Besides, it's *hot*," Rafi said.

"It's going to rain," I informed her.

"So?"

I sighed. "So, that dress is hideous," I finally confessed.

"It is not," Rafi said, looking at herself in the mirror on the back of my closet door.

I plopped down on my bed and told her about Michelle Snopes and Katie Lynn Howard, and the last Wednesday night that I'd spent at church.

When I finished, Rafi stuck her chin out, and said, "I'm wearing it."

"Aren't you scared?"

"Are Michelle and Katie Lynn burglars?" Rafi said.

"No."

"Then I'm not scared of them."

I was very impressed.

It must've shown, because Rafi added, "My mom says that when other kids pick on you, it doesn't really have anything to do with you. She says it means they feel bad about themselves, so they try to make someone else feel bad too."

Of course, I didn't believe Rafi so I chose a dress made of white eyelet, because I figured there was no way that white could be considered hideous. After all, white is defined as the absence of color.

Pate was sitting at the kitchen table eating scrambled eggs with ketchup when Rafi and I came downstairs. His mouth full, as always, he nodded at us.

He looked nice, I noticed. "Are you coming to church with us?"

Pate nodded again.

"Mama'll be happy," I told him.

I was pouring orange juice for Rafi and me when Daddy came into the kitchen — *not* wearing his pajamas. He was dressed for work, in a black suit. I was about to ask him where he was going. The courthouse is closed on Sundays, like just about everything else around here. But then I heard Mama's shoes clapping quickly down the hall. Her mouth dropped open when she saw Daddy.

He grinned at her. "I thought I'd drive you to church," he said, for the first time that I knew of.

I figured this was because of the thunder which rumbled again, closer now, causing the windows to rattle.

Then Daddy cleared his throat and added, "When the weather calls for it, I don't see why I couldn't give you a lift."

"Thank you," Mama said, hugging Daddy.

"But the truck's already parked," I said.

Orange juice spewed out of Pate's nose as he tried to control his laughter.

Mama snapped her fingers at the both of us. Two snaps over Daddy's shoulder, pointing her finger and giving us a slightly different version of her *Stop-It* or *Drop-It* look.

I knew she meant both: Pate was to *Stop it!* And I was to *Drop it!*

Honestly, I don't know how Daddy gets away with so much. No one questions Daddy, argues with him, or criticizes him in our house. And when he turns out to have been wrong about something, no one ever says anything like, "I told you so." I have no idea why or how this works (but I definitely plan to have the same arrangement with my family when I grow up).

When we arrived at church, Mama wanted to sit down front and Daddy wanted to sit in the back. So we ended up sitting in a pew in the middle of the new sanctuary, which smelled like paint.

At precisely 11:00 singing filled the sanctuary, but when I looked up, there was no one in the choir loft.

"Joyful, joyful,
We adore thee,
God of glory,
Lord of love . . ."

the choir sang as they entered the sanctuary from the back, and came down the aisles.

It was the coolest Call to Worship I had ever seen. (Call to Worship is fancy church language for *Hey, we're starting.*)

When the choir filled the choir loft and finished their song, Pastor Cooper got up and walked to the pulpit, which basically means *stage.*

"Wasn't that glorious?" Pastor Cooper said into

the microphone on the podium, clapping his hands and turning halfway to face the choir.

The congregation clapped, too.

When the applause died down, Pastor Cooper said again, "Glorious, just glorious! There's only one way it could've been better."

The sanctuary got quiet.

"Libby Morgan, where are you?" Pastor Cooper asked.

I thought about crawling under the pew in front of me, but decided I couldn't leave my best friend behind like that, especially not in that particular dress. So I forced myself to stay put, and instead fidgeted nervously with my BE FRI necklace.

When I glanced over at Mama, she had her hand raised high!

Pastor Cooper smiled down at her. "I don't mean to put you on the spot, Mrs. Morgan," he said, "but I surely do miss seeing your face up there in the choir loft."

I thought that maybe Pastor was going to ask Mama to consider rejoining the choir next week. But

Mama didn't wait. She hopped up off the pew and rushed down the aisle toward the choir loft.

I shrank in my seat.

Mrs. Peck turned and said something to the lady sitting next to her in the choir loft, and the lady moved down one seat.

Mama climbed the steps to the pulpit, wiggled her fingers at Pastor, and then hurried into the choir loft.

Mrs. Peck stood, hugged Mama, and pointed to the chair beside hers.

"Well, now, that's better isn't it?" Pastor Cooper said to the congregation. Without waiting for an answer, he said, "Let us pray."

After we prayed, the choir sang again.

Daddy leaned over and whispered, "Uh, Jamie Jo, does your mother know this song?"

I listened more closely. "I guess so. She sounds the same way she always does."

Daddy looked just the slightest bit worried.

Then Pastor Cooper began his sermon. "Turn in your Bibles to Hebrews, Chapter 13, Verse 5b, and read with me: *For God has said, 'Never will I leave you, never will I forsake you.'* And all of us here, we know that to be the truth, don't we?"

A chorus of "Amens" echoed through the sanctuary.

Pastor Cooper took off his glasses then, and began talking about how God had personally been with, and saved every person in our church from the explosion.

How come he didn't just save the church from the explosion? I wondered.

But as soon as the question popped into my head, Pastor Cooper tried to answer it. He said, "Now I don't presume to know what God's thinking, but if you want my best guess, here it is: God wanted to remind us of what's really important. He wanted to show us how much he loves each and every one of us. He wanted to show us how we're supposed to love each other, and forgive each other, no matter what, like he does."

I wanted to raise my hand and say, "Yes, but does he love us all *the same?*" But they don't take questions at church, at least not during the Sunday morning service. And anyway, I knew what Pastor Cooper would've said. I figured he'd say the same thing Mama always says, "Of course God loves us all the same!" This answer wouldn't be particularly helpful, seeing as how it only made me want to ask another question: But *how? How* could God possibly love us all the same? I mean, some people are good, and some people are bad. Some are nice, and some are just plain mean. So, how could God possibly love *all* of us, the nice ones and the mean ones, the same? And if he does, well . . . is that really fair?

To be honest, Pastor Cooper might've answered those questions that morning. I wouldn't know, because my mind tends to wander during his sermons. I try to pay attention. I *want* to pay attention. And every Sunday morning, I promise myself that I'll stay focused, that I'll listen to *every word.* But every Sunday morning, during the sermon, something happens (I have no idea what) and my thoughts can't help but wander.

So I wandered and I wondered: *What if no one had ever noticed Mama's singing, and they hadn't held auditions for choir? What if Pastor Cooper had never noticed*

Mama, and therefore never noticed her absence up there in the choir loft? What if Daddy had never noticed Mama, had never married her? What if Pate and I had never been born?

Maybe being noticed wasn't such a bad thing after all.

When I realized my thoughts had wandered again, I looked around the sanctuary, trying to tell if this was happening to anyone else. But as far as I could tell, it was just me. *What's wrong with me?* I wondered.

Then I peered over at Rafi beside me. Her mouth was hanging open and she blinked her eyes very, very slowly. Suddenly she pitched forward. She had fallen asleep! I felt so relieved that I wasn't the only one who'd stopped listening, that I wanted to hug her. But I poked her with my finger instead. I really hated to do it, because without the threat of burglars, Rafi seemed to be sleeping really good! But I was afraid she might start drooling or snoring or something, with her mouth hanging open like that.

Rafi jerked upright.

I smiled at her.

She smiled back, but her cheeks turned a deep pink and I knew she was embarrassed.

I sat up straight. *Stay focused,* I told myself.

The last thing I heard Pastor Cooper say was, "Remember, there is purpose in all things." Then he said, "Let us pray," and I knew that his sermon was over. I'd missed it. Again.

But everyone else (except for Rafi and me) must've been paying really close attention this morning, because things were somehow different when the service was over. People stood around crying and hugging each other. More than once, I heard, "I'm sorry," or "Please forgive me."

I turned to Rafi and said, "Sorry I had to wake you up like that, when you were sleeping so well. Hey, that reminds me, did I tell you that burglars are scared of dogs?"

"Seriously?" she said.

I nodded, and opened my mouth to tell Rafi exactly what Daddy (who'd actually known some burglars) had said, just as someone tapped me on the shoulder.

When I turned around, I was surprised, and a little terrified, to see Katie Lynn Howard and Michelle Snopes. I glanced over at Daddy, hoping that he would protect me.

But Daddy was talking to Mr. Wheeler, not paying any attention to me at all!

Suddenly, Michelle lurched toward me. I gulped at the air, and then her arms were around me.

"Wha . . . what are you doing?" I said, my arms pinned at my sides.

Michelle stepped back. "I'm hugging you," she said. "Duh."

"Oh," I said.

"I like your dress," Michelle said to Rafi.

"Yeah, me, too," Katie Lynn said.

"This is Michelle Snopes and Katie Lynn Howard," I told Rafi, giving her a look like, *It's them!!*

Rafi touched her *ST ENDS* necklace absently as she looked down at her dress. "Thanks," she said. "It's Jamie Jo's. She let me borrow it." She looked up at me then, like, *See? I told you it didn't have anything to do with the dress.*

154

I studied my sandals and waited for Michelle to say something like, *Actually, now that I'm really looking at it up close, that* is *the ugliest dress I've ever seen.*

But she didn't. Instead Michelle said, "Cool."

"Seriously," said Rafi.

Michelle and Katie Lynn nodded and then Michelle said, "Well, see ya."

"Yeah, see ya," Rafi said.

On the way home, Daddy said to Mama, "You sure sounded great this morning."

Mama laughed. "I did not."

Daddy smiled. "Well, you sure *looked* great up there. Very happy."

Mama nodded. "Do you think 'other people' thought so?"

Daddy thought about it while we all listened to the windshield wipers go back and forth in rhythm.

Finally, Daddy spoke. "Nobody can argue against that kind of happiness. That kind of happiness is like sunshine: It makes us all feel happy just to be in its warmth."

Then, Mama turned to Pate and said, "You're

looking awfully happy these days, son. Like sunshine yourself."

After we dropped Rafi off at her house, Mama turned to me. "I saw Miss Noel this morning, Jamie Jo."

I nodded.

"She said to tell you that she missed you at the last Bible study class, and she hopes you'll be able to make it this Wednesday, when choir practice and classes resume at church."

My stomach did a little somersault. In this instance, I have to admit that I wished Miss Noel hadn't noticed me *or* my absence.

"The way I see it, you have two choices," Mama said.

I looked up at her.

"You can either tell me what you were doing that night, which doesn't really make much difference now, or you can do the work you missed so that you'll be prepared this week."

"I'll do the work," I said immediately, feeling like I was getting away with something.

Mama nodded. "Today, at the kitchen table, while I make lunch."

Again I nodded.

"Are we going to sit here in the driveway all day or are we going inside?" Daddy asked.

I jumped out of the truck and sprinted toward the house before Daddy could ask any more questions.

After I changed clothes, I went downstairs with my Bible study workbook.

I found Daddy helping Mama in the kitchen. Another first, or near-first at least.

I sat down at the table and opened my workbook.

"Annie's coming home tomorrow," Mama said in a low voice as she stirred the pot on the stove.

I pretended to continue reading, but I was really listening.

Daddy didn't say anything.

"Pate wants to borrow the truck one night this week so he can take her out to dinner and show her around town — so much has changed since Annie lived here," Mama said.

Daddy still didn't say anything.

I was tempted to look up to try and read Daddy's face, but I decided I had better keep my eyes on my workbook.

When we were all seated at the table for lunch, Daddy said the prayer. Yet another first. When he finished, we all said, "Amen," and Mama started passing the tuna casserole around like nothing out of the ordinary had taken place, even though we all knew that it had. Pate and I just didn't want Mama to snap at us again.

"Pate, son," Daddy said gently, "don't you think it would be best if you concentrated fully on your studies?"

Oh no, I thought, *here we go.* But still, I took the opportunity, while all eyes were on Pate, to feed most of my tuna casserole to Buzz, who was sitting under the table.

"I'm makin' straight A's," Pate said, as in, *What more could you want?*

"Yes . . . Well, that's very good. It's just that Annie's our *neighbor,* and we don't have any intention

158

of moving. . . . So, if things don't work out. . ." Daddy let that thought hang in the air.

"Moving?" I said, my voice rising in panic. "Why would we move? We're not moving, ever, right? I mean, I *finally* have a best friend!" I held up my BE FRI necklace as proof.

Mama gave me a look, and put a finger over her lips to shush me.

Neither Pate nor Daddy seemed to have heard me anyway.

Pate set his fork down while there was still food on his plate. Yup, another first.

"Trust me this time, Dad," Pate said. "I know what I'm doing."

Daddy raised one eyebrow. "And how do you know?"

Pate thought for a few minutes while we all pretended to eat. Finally, he said, "I loved Sandy and Vicky. I'm not gonna say I didn't — but . . . well . . ."

"Yes?" Daddy said.

"I loved them because they made *me* happy, and I married them because I wanted to be happy."

Daddy nodded and chewed.

"But with Annie, well, it's different. I know we've only technically been dating for two months, but I feel like I really know her. I like making her laugh. I like making *her* happy because making *her* happy makes *me* feel happy — you know what I mean?"

Daddy set his fork down, too, and looked hard at Pate.

Uh oh, I thought, holding my breath.

"Son, I know *exactly* what you mean," Daddy said, smiling at Mama.

Mama smiled back.

I exhaled.

Pate nodded and picked up his fork.

Daddy picked up his fork, too.

Mama dabbed at her eyes with her napkin, and smiled the brightest smile, almost like she was singing on the inside.

"I'll wear the suit," I announced.

"What?" Daddy said, confused.

"I'll wear the suit to work when I grow up," I said. "Since Pate's probably going to marry the doctor."

It took Daddy a minute to catch up, but when he did, he burst out laughing. "Just be happy, Jamie Jo. That's all I ever really wanted for you and Pate, and I'm sorry if I led you to believe otherwise."

I looked at Pate like, *Did you hear that? He said he was sorry!*

I was pretty sure that this was another first.

Pate nodded and winked at me.

"Well," I said, "it would be great if you'd stop asking me about my spelling tests, Daddy. It was just the one time — and I was only in first grade."

"Yes, but think how *un*happy you'd be if you got another C," Daddy said.

"Take Buzz outside now, Jamie Jo," Mama said, "since he just finished eating *your* tuna casserole."

After lunch, Mama called Mrs. Peck and asked her if she could use some tomatoes. Mama had grown more tomatoes in her garden than we could eat, even with Pate at home.

When Mrs. Peck arrived, I opened the door.

"Hello, Jessie Jo," she said.

"Hey," I said flatly, wondering if she was going to call me Jessie Jo for the rest of my life.

I showed Mrs. Peck into the living room, where Mama was waiting for her.

As I turned to go, Mrs. Peck said, "Oh, Jessie Jo?"

"Ma'am?" I said, smiling sweetly. (Mama was watching.)

"If you and your friend, Rachel, from across the street, would like to come over and go swimming this afternoon after it clears up a little more, I'd be glad to have you."

This was possibly the best *first* of the day, as far as I was concerned. I broke into a real smile then, and said, "We'd love to! I'll just go call Rafi, Rachel, I mean."

That afternoon in Mrs. Peck's pool, I felt lighter than I ever had.

"Do you feel lighter?" I asked Rafi.

"Yeah," she said, "because I happen to be floating on water, and you are, too."

"Seriously," I said. "No, it's more than that."

"Yeah, I think I know what you mean. I do feel a

little lighter. I think it's because I don't feel as worried about burglars — I'm gonna let Crooner sleep in my room from now on."

"Yeah," I said, "and I don't have to worry as much about bees, or being noticed — I'm just not as afraid as I used to be somehow, only a little afraid."

"Seriously," Rafi said. "Hey, I know! We'll make a pact!

"What kind of pact?"

Rafi thought for a minute, and then said, "I'll leave my bedroom door cracked open tonight, if you'll leave your flyswatter zipped up in your backpack when you walk to my house in the morning."

I tried to think how long it would take me to get my flyswatter out of my backpack in a street-crossing emergency. I figured about six seconds. "Deal," I said. "But how will we know *for sure* that we both did it?"

"We're best friends!" Rafi shrieked, splashing me.

I laughed and splashed her back.

Thunder rumbled heavily, in the distance, the way it had this morning, just before the sky opened up and poured rain.

Rafi and I both looked up at the rain clouds moving in.

"Aw, shoot, now what are we gonna do?" Rafi half-whined.

"We have a lot of Scotch tape at my house."

A Note from the Author

I receive a great number of forwarded emails on any given day—everything from urgent warnings to messages of hope. But no matter how tempted I am to delete without reading, I read them all. Often, I check these forwarded emails for truth and accuracy at www.snopes.com, where I learned that aspartame hasn't, in fact, caused a cancer epidemic; Glade Plug-Ins haven't, in fact, been responsible for starting thousands of house fires; and, much to my disappointment, neither Bill Gates, nor Microsoft, nor AOL is giving away free cash and merchandise to people who forward emails (shoot!).

So, imagine my surprise to learn that a forwarded "message of hope," which seemed altogether impossible, was indeed factual. These are the facts:

- Choir practice at the West Side Baptist Church in Beatrice, Nebraska, always began promptly at 7:20 on Wednesday nights.
- At 7:25 on Wednesday evening, March 1st, 1950, West Side Baptist Church exploded with such tremendous power that a nearby radio station was forced off the air and windows in surrounding houses were shattered.
- Nevertheless, none of the church's fifteen choir members were harmed, because none had yet arrived for choir practice — they were all running late that night.

Can you imagine? Well, I tried. And the more I thought about it, the more it seemed something worth singing (or writing) about, so I did. I wrote for my daughter, Laurel Grace, who was ten years old at the time. I thought that Laurel Grace would appreciate the story more than most, because she has the kind of unwavering faith in God, in people, and in me, that both inspires and humbles me. In addition, I couldn't think of a group of people more in need of a "message of hope" than middle-graders! Okay, okay, so I am judging by my own middle school experience, and it was a little rough (read: horrific); I'm sure yours is going just fine. You look fine. Your hair is fine. Your teeth are fine. You are fine. Really.

For more information on these events, visit: www.snopes.com/luck/choir.htm.

Acknowledgments

First and foremost, I thank God, who has blessed me in more ways than I could ever hope to be deserving of, beginning—but certainly not ending—with my family.

Thanks to my entire family, all of whom are truly amazing individuals that I would have been blessed just to encounter in life: Being part of your family remains, as always, a great source of honor, pride, and inspiration.

Special thanks to my father, David, The Giant, and to my lifelong friend, Janet.

Special thanks to my mother, Ann, the sweet songbird, and to her husband, Frank, for loving her so.

Thank you, thank you, thank you to my sisters,

who embody the true meaning of the word in every way: Sarah Clark, Robin Pickett, and Leslie R. Smith.

To Marie Stopher, the lovely librarian who provided me with *Eetookashoo* — the first picture book of my memory—and other favorites: My love and thanks for this, and so, so much more.

To Ruth Lanphear, a beautiful writer and an even more glorious friend, who believed in me long before I offered much of anything to believe in: I miss you every day.

To my husband, Mark, who has given me a life and a love far beyond anything I would have ever dared to hope for: Mere words could never convey my love, gratitude, respect, and admiration, for the wonderful husband, father, friend, and human being that you are.

To my daughter, Laurel Grace, without whom I never would've found my place, in so many ways: You are my reason for being, for doing, for hoping, and for believing.

Thanks to my aunt Janet, a brilliant author, who (eventually) left the safety of her basement during a

tornado, to answer the insistent ringing of her tele-
phone, and to console me when I received the first of
many, many painful rejection letters, and who just
kept saying, "You, my dear niece, are a writer—so
write!"

Thanks to my aunt Nancy, who told me repeat-
edly, "You have a gift and you must not diminish it in
any way."

Thanks to Michael Carr and J. D. Miller, both of
whom taught me much about writing, by slipping
learning in between laughs, the way parents slip
diced carrots in between the folds of ravioli.

A million thanks to Kathleen McAfee and Joyce
Payne, both of whom are always ready and willing to
read for me—immediately.

Unending gratitude and admiration to Lorri Hare,
Deana Wehr, and everyone at the Bowling Green War-
ren County Humane Society in Kentucky, for doing
the quiet work of angels, and for providing me with
the perfect co-writer and companion: a big, floppy
mutt that sits faithfully at my feet as I write and
rewrite page after page—she never gives up on me!

Special thanks to two fabulous friends and neighbors (and occasional storytellers): Ralph Delmotte and Eve Petty.

I will always be indebted to the patron saint of editors, Shannon White, who (miraculously) plucked me from the slush pile and worked tirelessly alongside me, until this novel seemed maybe, just possibly, perhaps, worthy of the plucking.

To Lara Sissell, Noelle Pederson, and all the other marvelous minds at Eerdmans Books for Young Readers: Thank you for the investment of your time, talent, and, above all, faith.

Finally, my love and appreciation to Pastor Bob Cook and the people of The Church at Grace Park, in White House, Tennessee, who provided me with an incredibly loving extended family, and a home away from home.